"Reckon you know what I'm gonna ask," Lonny sighed. "Are you a regulator, fella?"

"No," Clint replied. "I'm just a traveling gunsmith who came to town on business."

"Shit," Pedro growled. "Nobody would come to this lump of horse dung if he wanted to make money. Not unless this *hombre* is a stinkin' bounty hunter."

"Pedro is right," Jed agreed. "You don't figure this jasper would admit it if'n he was a regulator, do you?"

"Wait a minute," Lonny urged. "Somethin' about this fella seems familiar. What's your name, stranger?"

"Clint Adams," the Gunsmith replied mildly.

All three outlaws stared at the Gunsmith as if he had just grown another head . . .

Don't miss any of the lusty, hard riding action in the Charter Western series, THE GUNSMITH:

And coming next month:

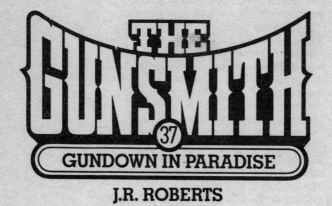

THE GUNSMITH

37

GUNDOWN IN PARADISE

J.R. ROBERTS

CHARTER BOOKS, NEW YORK

THE GUNSMITH #37: GUNDOWN IN PARADISE

A Charter Book / published by arrangement with
the author

PRINTING HISTORY
Charter Original / February 1985

ISBN: 0-441-30935-6

Charter Books are published by The Berkley Publishing Group,
200 Madison Avenue, New York, New York 10016.
PRINTED IN THE UNITED STATES OF AMERICA

Dedicated to
Mark Mandell

GUNDOWN IN PARADISE

ONE

Clint Adams had come to a decision. He had been in Piercetown for less than two hours and he had already decided it wasn't much of a town. Every building was made of wood. It looked so flimsy Clint reckoned a strong wind would blow the entire town apart.

Clint had driven his wagon into town. The vehicle was Clint's home on wheels, a mobile business which contained all his worldly possessions. Clint was a traveling gunsmith; he roamed the American West, going from territory to territory, town to town, making a living by repairing and modifying firearms.

However, Clint Adams had been known as the Gunsmith even before he had chosen the occupation. The monicker had been given to him by a sensationalist newspaper journalist who had begun work on an article about the then Deputy Sheriff Clint Adams. The writer learned that the young lawman had converted a regular .45-caliber Colt revolver to fire double-action.

At the time, a double-action or self-cocking revolver

was a rarity in the American West. Most guns were still single-action requiring the owner to cock the hammer before firing a shot. Clint's modification was unique, and he had already earned a reputation as a lightning-fast gunman. Thus, the newspaper man labeled him "the Gunsmith" and the title plagued Clint for the rest of his life.

After eighteen years as a lawman, Clint Adams turned in his badge and vowed never to wear one again. He decided to wander the West with his traveling gunsmith shop. However, Clint's retirement had been anything but restful.

The Gunsmith continued to find himself in the middle of dangerous situations. He wasn't quite certain why this happened. Of course, his reputation as a gunman had grown. Oddly enough, the stories about the Gunsmith were usually understated. The man's true adventures were far more incredible than all the myths. Yet the legend of the Gunsmith was enough to cause him ample headaches from young gunslingers in search of a reputation.

However, often Clint's natural curiosity led him into trouble. The Gunsmith could never resist a beautiful girl, a game of chance or an unsolved mystery. All three had caused him considerable trouble in the past, yet Clint always seemed to find a way to justify any risks he decided to take.

There didn't seem to be much opportunity to get into trouble in Piercetown. Didn't seem to be much opportunity to make a profit either. The Oklahoma Territory had formerly been Indian land, and it remained a haven for half-breeds who moved to Oklahoma to escape the prejudice and discrimination found throughout the rest of the nation.

GUNDOWN IN PARADISE

Clint Adams wasn't a bigot; he didn't judge a man by the color of his skin or his ethnic background. But half-breeds were suspicious of strangers, and although the residents of Piercetown did not have a local gunsmith, they were still leery of doing business with Clint.

The Gunsmith didn't think this was due to his reputation as a gunman. Following a personal custom, Clint had visited the local sheriff's office when he arrived in town. The Gunsmith had been a lawman long enough to realize anyone who wears a badge appreciates knowing about strangers in town. Especially someone with a reputation like his.

Sheriff Harrimon Greyelk didn't seem to care who Clint Adams might be. The poker-faced lawman quietly listened to the Gunsmith explain who he was and why he was in Piercetown. Greyelk nodded, casually gazing over the tall, lean stranger.

Clint Adams was a pleasant looking man, although he appeared a bit scruffy after spending almost a month on the trail. With twenty days of whiskers on his face and plenty of trail dust on his clothes, the Gunsmith might easily be mistaken for a simple saddle-bum. Greyelk noticed the jagged scar on Clint's left cheek. A tattoo of violence. It was only one of the many scars which marred the Gunsmith's body.

Of course, anyone can receive a scar. Greyelk was more interested in the Colt Clint wore low on his right hip. The hammer was wide to make it easier to cock. Even a double-action revolver is most accurate when fired in single-action. The metal was clean and recently oiled, evidence the owner took excellent care of his gun. The holster had been molded to suit the pistol.

"You're a gunfighter," Greyelk declared. He was not

asking a question, merely stating a fact.

"No," Clint corrected. "I'm just a traveling gunsmith looking for some business. Trying to make an honest dollar."

"You carry that gun like a man who is used to killing with one," Greyelk insisted. "All sorts of outlaws escaped to the Oklahoma Territory. The Missouri pistolmen headed for Texas after the War Between the States. Then they figured Oklahoma was a safer place to run to."

"I'm not a gunman," Clint sighed. For once he was sorry to encounter someone who was unfamiliar with the "legend" of the Gunsmith. "In fact, I used to be a lawman myself."

"Who you are, or what you were in the past don't concern me," the solemn faced sheriff replied, "as long as you cause no harm to anyone in my town. If you fix guns for money, that's fine with me. Just don't cause any trouble, Mr. Adams."

"I'm not looking for any trouble," Clint assured him.

"Just remember I am the law in Piercetown," Greyelk warned. "Maybe you used to be a lawman, but you don't wear a badge now. Remember that."

"It's been a pleasure to meet you too, Sheriff," the Gunsmith said dryly.

After paying his social call on the sheriff, Clint took his wagon to the local livery stable. A tall, painfully thin figure greeted him at the front of the building. Greet might be too strong a term for the reception Clint received. The tall scarecrow stood with his arms folded on his chest and solemnly nodded at the Gunsmith.

"I am called Charlie Spotted-Horse," the man announced as if he expected Clint to recognize his name.

"You want to use my livery, stranger?"

The Gunsmith resisted an urge to smile. Charlie Spotted-Horse wore a formal black suit which would have been more appropriate on an undertaker than a hostler. A stovepipe hat was perched on the man's head. Two hawk feathers jutted from the hatband. Charlie resembled an Indian version of Abe Lincoln.

Yet Charlie displayed an eccentric dignity as he stood erect, trying to impress Clint with his own importance. Charlie's copper-brown skin was as wrinkled as worn parchment, and the hair under his hat was iron-gray. Charlie had seen many summers, almost twice the number Clint had lived through in forty-odd years. A man learns many things in such a long lifetime, including the necessity of being proud of his own station in life.

Charlie Spotted-Horse owned the livery stable. The aged half-breed clearly took great pride in this. Clint respected Charlie for this. A man who realizes what he is and stands tall when he speaks of his profession, is usually the best in his field. Such a man should not be taken lightly.

"Pleased to make your acquaintance," Clint replied. "I'd be obliged if you'd look after my wagon and horses. Especially Duke. I'll pay you well for giving them special consideration, friend."

"I do not need extra money to be trusted to take good care of your possessions," Charlie declared.

"But extra work deserves extra payment," Clint insisted. "This wagon is all I have, and Duke means more to me than anything short of my own life."

"Duke?" the hostler frowned.

Clint moved to the rear of his wagon and untied Duke.

A magnificent solid black Arabian gelding, Duke was not only the most beautiful horse Clint had ever owned, he was also the fastest, strongest, and smartest. The Gunsmith and Duke had been together since the animal was a yearling colt. They were friends, companions, and partners.

Charlie Spotted-Horse gazed at Duke in obvious appreciation of the long, smooth muscles of the superb animal. The half-breed recognized the almost human intelligence reflected in the horse's large brown eyes. He immediately realized that Duke was indeed something very special.

"That's a nice horse," Charlie said, trying to reclaim his impassive professional mask. "Maybe I should get paid more for looking after him."

"What's your regular fee?" the Gunsmith inquired.

"Fifty cents a day," Charlie answered. "But I'll have to charge you seventy-five because that wagon will take up a lot of room."

"I'll pay you double," Clint stated. "Just make sure you treat Duke to the very best you've got in there. I want him fed and watered. Brush him down real good too. And I don't want any of my animals in a drafty stall."

"I shall see to all this, Mr.—?"

"Adams. Clint Adams."

"You are the one they call the Gunsmith?" Charlie inquired, his tone almost reverent.

"*They* do call me that," Clint replied with a sigh, "whoever *they* are. I call myself Clint, and I'd be obliged if you'd do likewise, friend."

"It is said you are a great warrior with a six-gun," the half-breed remarked. "But it is also said you are a man of honor. Your enemies have great cause to fear you, but a good person in need can turn to you for help."

"Don't believe everything you hear, fella," the Gunsmith urged. "And don't mistake me for some sort of righteous do-gooder. I came to Piercetown to try to rustle up some money as a gunsmith—and by that I mean repairing folks' guns for a profit. I'm not spoiling for a fight."

"Your destiny may decide otherwise, Clint," Charlie said solemnly.

"All I want my destiny to do is send me enough customers to make my trip worthwhile," Clint declared.

"In that case," Charlie sighed, "I wish you luck. You shall need it in this town."

The Gunsmith understood what the hostler meant. He hadn't seen more than four people since he rode into Piercetown. Besides Sheriff Greyelk and Charlie Spotted-Horse, Clint had noticed an old woman seated in a rocking chair on a front porch and a portly man sweeping the plankwalk in front of his shop.

Having settled Duke and his rig, Clint headed for the local saloon. Experience had taught him saloons were the best places to strike up a friendly conversation with strangers. He had generally found them to be a good way to find potential customers as well. Besides, he was thirsty.

The saloon didn't appear to have a name. If it hadn't had batwing doors, Clint wouldn't have known what the building was. The interior was very plain. The tables and chairs appeared to be made of apple-crate wood and chicken wire. A long, wide board nailed across the top of rain barrels formed the bar. Dirty, dark-brown sawdust covered the floor. It smelled of sweat, spit, and stale beer.

A fat man sat on a stool behind the bar. His hands were

folded on his paunchy gut, and his back was propped against a wall. The fellow snored so hard Clint was surprised he didn't wake himself up. There was no one else in the saloon.

Clint was almost afraid to wake the bartender, afraid the fellow might fall off his stool. The Gunsmith approached the counter and gently rapped his knuckles on the wood.

"Huh?" the bartender uttered, his eyes snapping open. "Oh, good afternoon . . . uh, I don't think I know you."

"No," the Gunsmith confirmed, wondering if the man was nearsighted or drunk. "I'm a stranger in town."

"You get off the stagecoach, Mr.—?"

"Just call me Clint," the Gunsmith replied. "I rode into Piercetown in my wagon. Didn't even know the stage goes through here."

"Sure does," the bartender nodded. "Lucky for me, too. Most of my customers are folks passin' through on the stage."

"That doesn't sound so good for me," Clint muttered.

"Oh, I got some real fine liquor here," the bartender declared quickly. "Got a couple bottles of Kentucky sour mash and some red-eye whiskey."

"A beer will be fine," the Gunsmith told him.

"Yes, sir." The bartender bowed his head as he put a glass mug under the tap of a beer keg. "Reckon you'll be in town long, Clyde?"

"Doesn't look like it," the Gunsmith sighed. "And my name's Clint."

"Sure enough," the bartender said as he placed the beer mug on the counter. "Here you go, Clyde."

"Thanks," Clint replied. He didn't bother to correct him about his name.

The batwings opened, and three men entered. The trio wore ill-treated denim and mud-caked boots. One man had a battered Mexican sombrero on his head. The other two wore stetsons which appeared to be in the same wretched condition.

Clint noticed all three wore gunbelts. The squat, bearded man with the sombrero also carried a large bowie knife at the small of his back. One of his companions, a tall, wiry jasper, had a Winchester carbine leaning on a shoulder. The third, a beefy, muscular man, packed a Remington revolver in a cross-draw position on his belt.

"Get us a bottle of red-eye, toad face," the beefy man ordered.

"Sure, Lonny," the bartender nodded as if he wanted to cave in his breastbone by hitting it repeatedly with his chin.

"Surely wish there was some other town 'round these parts," the rifleman muttered. "Hate comin' into a place what's crawlin' with goddamn Injuns."

"Hell, Jed," the bearded man laughed. "If the big bad redskins try to scalp you, I'll protect you."

"Shit on you, Pedro," Jed spat a glob of snotty saliva on the floor. "You Mexicans is all part Injun. You'd probably help them lift my hair."

"I ain't no Injun," Pedro hissed. "I told you the stinkin' Yaqui killed my father. You say somethin' like that again, I'll cut your *cajones* off and feed 'em to you."

"Take it easy," Lonny, the big man, urged. "It's a hot day, and none of us feel too good. Don't let that get you two fightin' with each other. Blackie would cut off both *your* balls if he knew how you been carryin' on."

"Here's your whiskey, gents," the bartender announced, placing a bottle on the counter.

"Put it on credit," Jed sneered. "Blackie's credit is still good here, ain't it?"

"Sure," the bartender assured him. "Blackie's credit is always good with me."

The Gunsmith had a suspicion who Blackie might be. An outlaw named Edward Black had raised a lot of hell a couple years before. Black led a band of cutthroat hootowls who robbed enough banks and farmhouses in Kansas to get a $2,000 price on their collective heads. Blackie was worth $1,000 all by himself.

The gang had disappeared some time ago. Clint followed Blackie's career with only passing interest, but he recalled rumors about how the outlaws must have headed for Texas or even Mexico. Or Indian territory in Oklahoma.

"Hey," Pedro snapped, his eyes locked on Clint Adams. "I don't think I've ever seen you before."

"Not in Piercetown anyway," Jed agreed. He cocked his head as he examined the Gunsmith's face. "Somethin' seems mighty familiar about him though. Reckon it might be that scar."

Jed gripped the lever of his Winchester as he spoke. Pedro's hand rested on the butt of his Colt revolver. The Gunsmith seemed relaxed despite their open hostility, but he drank the beer with his left hand while his right hand dangled near the modified double-action revolver on his hip.

"You boys are gettin' a bit too edgy," Lonny declared. "This here fella ain't doin' us no harm. Let's not jump to conclusions. Blackie don't want us stirrin' up bad feelin' in this town. Killin' a man what we had no call killin' ain't gonna make us none too popular 'round here.''

"But killin' a goddamn bounty hunter would be self-defense," Jed insisted, his eyes glaring at Clint.

"Now, there you got a point, Jed," Lonny agreed. He turned to the Gunsmith. "I figure you must be sort of concerned about all this, fella."

"You might say that," Clint admitted.

"Reckon you know what I'm gonna ask," Lonny sighed. "Are you a regulator, fella?"

"No," Clint replied. "I'm just a traveling gunsmith who came to town on business."

"Shit," Pedro growled. "Nobody would come to this lump of horse dung if he wanted to make money. Not unless this *hombre* is a stinkin' bounty hunter."

"Pedro is right," Jed agreed. "You don't figure this jasper would admit it if'n he was a regulator, do you?"

"Wait a minute," Lonny urged. "Somethin' about this fella seems familiar. What's your name, stranger?"

"Clint Adams," the Gunsmith replied mildly.

All three outlaws stared at him as if he had just grown another head. Jed backed away from Clint. Pedro moved to the left. Clint realized if the trio decided to draw against him, they'd fan out. Multiple targets are more difficult to deal with when they aren't bunched together.

"Hold on, fella," Lonny warned. "Ain't no point in us shootin' holes in each other unless we absolutely have to. Now, I ain't heard nothin' about the Gunsmith bein' no bounty hunter. Could be he's just here tryin' to strike up some business a fixin' guns. I hear that's what he does most of the time to make hisself a livin'."

"Yeah," Jed said tensely. "Well, I reckon that's possible."

"Look," Clint began. "I'm not interested in what you fellas are doing. Personally, I think all three of you are rude, loud-mouth hardcases, but that isn't a good enough reason to kill you."

All three outlaws stiffened, but none of them reached for a weapon. The bartender smiled, pleased that the trio had met somebody who could push them around for a change.

"We ain't got no quarrel with you neither, Adams," Lonny sniveled.

"That's good," the Gunsmith replied simply. "Keep it that way and you'll get to live a lot longer."

TWO

The Gunsmith moved to a table and sat with his back to the wall. Clint quietly sipped his beer, watching the three outlaws just in case one of them decided to try to take him on when it looked like he dropped his guard. The Gunsmith didn't think any of them were that stupid or that short-tempered, but he had learned never to underestimate the stupidity of outlaws.

Clint Adams had been a lawman for eighteen years, and he realized that most men turn to a life of crime because they're simply too dumb and lazy to work for a living. Most outlaws were illiterate, and damn few were clever enough to plan anything more complicated than wave a gun, grab the money and run. Even the most successful hootowls tended to spend their money on liquor, loose women, and poker. When it ran out, they'd go steal some more.

Yet, although most outlaws were dumber than house bricks, they remained an unpredictable breed. Since human life meant little if anything to such cutthroats, one could never be certain what might rub them the wrong way, or how much it might take to get them mad enough to try to kill you. However, the law of the jungle was an outlaw's creed. The first rule is survival. Damn few gunmen will take an unnecessary risk unless they figured to make a profit in the process.

Clint was also certain the three gunhawks wouldn't want to do anything which might upset their boss, Edward Black. The Gunsmith wondered where Blackie's gang was holed up. He didn't ponder this too much since the outlaws weren't his problem—at least, not yet.

The thunder of horse hoofs and the rattle of wagon-wheel spokes announced the arrival of the stagecoach. The bartender quickly began to wipe off his counter. Lonny, Jed, and Pedro turned to gaze out the batwings. Clint continued to drink his beer unconcerned about the stage.

"Why I'll be dipped in cow manure," Jed chuckled. "Look at what just stepped offa' the ol' Concorde."

"Ain't seen a dude like that since I left Baltimore," Lonny added with amusement. "Probably a whiskey drummer."

"Better not be another flim-flam varmint," the bartender remarked. "Last one of them drummers sold me a case of red-eye. Let me sample one bottle, and it was mighty fine liquor, but all the other bottles was filled with water."

"*Madre de Dios*," Pedro whistled. "Now that is a fine-looking woman."

"Dude's helpin' her outta the coach," Jed remarked, craning his neck to try to get a better look at the passengers. "Wonder if'n she's his wife."

"Well, lookie here," Lonny smiled. "He's headed this way. Reckon we can find out whether that gal's his woman or not."

Clint hadn't paid much attention to their conversation until he heard them mention a woman. The Gunsmith hadn't had a woman for a long time—too long, in Clint's opinion. He had been on the trail for over a month, and he hadn't met a willing woman since he left Texas.

The batwings parted and a tall, lean figure crossed the threshold. Clint's eyes widened with surprise when he recognized the lean, handsome face of the new arrival to Piercetown.

"Marcel Duboir," the Gunsmith whispered, barely able to believe what he saw.

But he knew he couldn't mistake anyone else for the dashing, flamboyant young Frenchman. Marcel wore a dark, blue-and-white pinstripe suit, a red cravat with a gold tiepin and a derby. A brass-handled walking stick was held in his left fist.

Marcel looked as fancy as a San Francisco whorehouse, but Clint knew there was more to the Frenchman than his flashy appearance. Duboir was an intelligent, worldly man. The blacksheep of a respected family in the French Quarter of New Orleans, Marcel was the son of a retired judge who had dared to take on the powerful criminal syndicate run by Gaston Lacombe.

Clint Adams had found himself in the middle of a war between the judge and Lacombe. Choosing sides had been easy. The Gunsmith fought alongside Judge Duboir's people. Marcel proved to be his greatest ally. The younger Duboir was fearless in battle and ten times tougher than his polished exterior suggested. Clint and Marcel had been a formidable combination. Two very different men in many ways, yet both were courageous, skillful fighters who shared a common interest in beautiful women and challenging adventures.

But what the hell was Marcel Duboir doing in an obscure little town like Piercetown, Oklahoma? The Frenchman looked as out of place in the shoddy little saloon as a pink bow on a boar hog.

"*Bonjour*," Marcel greeted the bartender as he approached the counter. "That is, hello. How are you today, *Monsieur?*"

"I ain't buyin' no whiskey," the bartender declared in a hard voice, mistaking Marcel for a drummer.

"But I am not selling anything," the Frenchman assured him. "Indeed, I came in here to buy a drink from you, *oui?*"

"Oh," the bartender shrugged. "Well, that's different. What'll it be, fella?"

"A glass of sherry would be fine," Marcel replied. "That is, if you have something dry, but not too tart. Otherwise, a dollop of brandy would—"

"Are you tryin' to be funny?" the bartender demanded.

"Sure looks mighty funny to me," Jed snorted, strolling over to Marcel. "Look like maybe you're one of them she-boys—the type that likes men. That so, Frenchy?"

"Hardly, *Monsieur*," Duboir answered, tapping his palm with the cane. "You seem to be trying to insult me, yet I have done you no harm. Why do you act so strangely? Did your mother drop you on your fat, ugly head when you were a boy?"

"Why you peacock son of a bitch," Jed growled, about to swing his rifle from his shoulder.

Clint prepared to rise from his chair, his hand on the grips of his modified Colt revolver. Lonny stepped forward and grabbed Jed's Winchester. He yanked it from the young hootowl's grasp and slammed the carbine on the bar. Clint winced, half-expecting the impact to jar the hammer forward to fire the weapon. These fellas are too dumb to carry guns, he thought.

"Hold on, Jed," Lonny told his partner. "This dude ain't heeled. Can't go swinging an iron at some greenhorn what ain't armed."

"Hey, *hombre*," Pedro began. "That woman who got off the stage with you, is she your wife?"

"No, *Monsieur*," Marcel smiled at the Mexican outlaw. "But she is a beauty, *oui*? I could write a poem about that lovely and charming—"

"Shut up, you fancy-mouthed bastard!" Jed snarled. "Since you ain't man enough to carry a gun, I reckon I'm gonna have to settle for just beatin' the shit out of you."

"I wouldn't advise you to try that, fella," the Gunsmith warned as he rose from his chair once more.

"*Merde alors!*" Marcel exclaimed when he noticed Clint for the first time. "*L'armurier! Comment allez-vous, mon ami!*"

Jed figured Marcel was distracted so he chose that moment to launch his attack. He swung a wild right cross at the Frenchman's smiling face.

Marcel's cane rose swiftly and knocked the attacking arm aside. Jed staggered off balance, and Marcel's foot snapped a *savate* kick to the outlaw's midsection. Jed groaned and doubled up. The Frenchman stamped a foot into the back of his knee. The gunhawk's leg buckled, and he fell to all fours.

Duboir gracefully pivoted and unleashed a side-kick which struck Jed between the shoulder blades. The outlaw was propelled forward by the kick and landed head-first against the frame of the bar. He slumped to the dirty floor in a dazed heap.

"Cabron!" Pedro hissed as he seized Marcel's arms from behind.

"You fight mighty dirty, dude," Lonny snarled as he stepped forward and cocked back a fist.

"Oui," Marcel replied. Then he kicked Lonny in the balls.

The big man howled and staggered backward, clutching his battered crotch with both hands. Marcel quickly stomped on Pedro's instep. The Mexican yelped in pain and shifted his foot out of the way, still holding Marcel's arms from behind.

The Frenchman executed a short rear-kick and drove the back of his heel between Pedro's splayed legs. The outlaw gasped in agony. Marcel broke free of the Mexican's hold and slashed the brass handle of his cane across Pedro's face. The Mexican crashed to the floor.

"Goddamn it," Lonny rasped through clenched teeth as he reached for the revolver on his belt.

"Draw that gun, and I'll blow your brains out before you get a chance to use it," the Gunsmith warned.

Clint had drawn his Colt and aimed it at the outlaw's head. He cocked the hammer. The double-action weapon didn't need to be cocked, but the ominous click of the hammer locking back is a sound that never fails to get one's attention.

"What the hell?" Lonny turned and glared at the Gunsmith. "This ain't none of your business, Adams."

"When two fellas try to beat up one man," Clint began, "I figure I ought to step in and stop it. Especially when you decide to draw a gun on an unarmed man who happens to be a friend of mine."

"Aw, shit," Lonny growled.

"I wondered how long you would just sit and watch the fight," Marcel remarked cheerfully.

"You didn't look like you needed any help," Clint replied.

"With clumsy trash like this?" the Frenchman scoffed. "Certainly not, *mon ami*."

"All right, Adams," Lonny stated as he unbuckled his gunbelt. "You want to get involved in this? Then put down your gun, and we'll go at it hand-to-hand."

"Damn," Clint sighed, but he placed his Colt on the table. "You fellas are real gluttons for punishment, aren't you?"

Lonny uttered a bestial roar which resembled the sound a grizzly bear might make if someone shoved a hot iron up its ass. He charged the Gunsmith, obviously planning to overpower him by his superior size and weight.

Clint whirled away from the bar, holding a chair in both hands. He adroitly hurled the chair in a low arch and let it go. Furniture skidded across the floor and struck Lonny's shins. The chair clipped his feet out from under him. The big man fell face first with an enraged grunt, terminated when his jawbone hit the floor.

The Gunsmith dashed forward as Lonny began to rise. Clint hit him with a solid right and knocked the outlaw on his back. Lonny sighed as consciousness was expelled from his body like air from a leaky balloon.

The Gunsmith rose and walked to his table. He returned the .45 Colt to leather and gathered up his beer mug.

"Jesus," the bartender croaked hoarsely.

"What are you upset about?" Clint asked. "At least nobody got killed."

Suddenly, both Jed and Pedro sprang up from the floor. Jed had drawn his sidearm and aimed the revolver at the Gunsmith while Pedro dragged his bowie knife from its sheath and attacked Marcel Duboir.

Clint's modified Colt appeared in his hand as if by magic. He snap-aimed and fired the double-action pistol before Jed could cock his gun. A 230-grain lead slug smashed into Jed's chest, left of center and drilled through his heart. The outlaw collapsed, the unfired six-shooter still in his fist.

Marcel twisted the handle of his walking stick and rapidly drew a two-and-a-half-foot blade from the hollow scabbard of his cane. He met Pedro's lunge with a fencer's thrust. The point of his sword was just as accurate and lethal as the Gunsmith's bullet. Pedro wilted to the floor, blood squirting from his punctured heart.

"Uh," Clint began, giving a short apologetic shrug. "At least nobody got killed until now."

THREE

"I knew there would be trouble from you," Sheriff Greyelk said grimly as he gazed down at the corpses of Pedro and Jed.

"But I just arrived on the stage," Marcel Duboir replied with a tone of confusion in his voice.

"I think the sheriff was talking about me," Clint Adams commented.

Greyelk had heard the gunshot within the saloon and arrived seconds later, a double-barreled Greener in his fists. The lawman parted the batwings and stepped inside, sadly shaking his head with despair.

"Clint Adams," Greyelk addressed the Gunsmith. "You are under arrest."

"Like hell I am," Clint replied gruffly. "That son of a bitch tried to kill me. What was I supposed to do? Let him take a shot at me and try to catch the bullet in my teeth?"

"Excuse me, Sheriff?" Marcel began. "Good afternoon, I'm Marcel Duboir."

"I will get your statement later," Greyelk told him.

"I just wanted to explain that I killed that man," Duboir said, pointing at Pedro's body with the tip of his cane.

"What?" Greyelk blinked with surprise. He turned to the bartender. "Harlan, can you make heads or tails of what the hell is goin' on here?"

"Sure, Sheriff," the bartender nodded. "Those three fellas are members—"

"What three fellas?" Greyelk sighed.

"Oh, the two that are dead now and that third fella over there who Clyde knocked out." Harlan pointed at Lonny's unconscious form.

"All right," the sheriff began. "Now who the hell is Clyde?"

"He means me," Clint explained.

"Yeah," Harlan agreed. "Clyde here knocked that fella out. Fella's name is Lonny Sterling, and he and the two other jaspers is members of Ed Black's gang. Well, I reckon the dead men ain't outlaws no more, but they was part of Blackie's bunch afore they got killed."

"Harlan," the sheriff began in an exhausted tone. "Who started the trouble?"

"Oh, Blackie's bunch did," the bartender answered. "They was spoiling for a fight as soon as they come in here. All three of 'em jumped this French fella. He kicked the bejesus outta 'em too. And I mean that literal. Ain't never seen a man use his feet so fast in a fight."

"My style is called *savate*," Marcel announced cheerfully. "It is a form of French kick-boxing. I'm so glad you like it, *Monsieur*."

"You just hush up, damn it!" Greyelk snapped. "Harlan, what happened after the Frenchman beat these fellas up?''

"Lonny pulled a gun," Harlan replied. "That's when Clyde got into the ruckus. He beat the hell out of Lonny. Then Pedro and Jed attacked Clyde and the Frenchy with weapons. They had to defend themselves, I reckon. Sure was fast. Clyde shot down Jed quicker than you can say 'gaddamn Sherman.' Frenchy stabbed the Mex with his pig-sticker just about as quick."

"Pig-sticker?" Greyelk turned to Marcel.

"My cane sword," Marcel explained. He turned the handle of his walking stick and pulled the blade out far enough to expose a foot of polished steel. "But I assure you I would not use it to stick pigs with. This happens to be a very fine and expensive sword. It is made of Toledo steel, the very best Spanish metal. Although we French are the finest swordsmen in the world, the Spanish make the best swords. Hard to believe, but true."

"You sure you didn't just talk that fella to death?" Greyelk asked with a sneer.

"Quite sure," Marcel replied.

"Look, Sheriff," the Gunsmith began. "Marcel and I acted in self-defense. These three bastards are outlaws and you know it. Why don't you wake Lonny up and throw his ass in jail?"

"I don't need you tellin' me how to do my job, Adams," Greyelk said fiercely.

"Harlan recognized those three," Clint continued. "They've been here before, probably bullying and bad-mouthing folks just like they did today. Don't tell me you never noticed them before, Sheriff. What it gets down to is you've tolerated their bullshit because you don't want a confrontation with Blackie's gang.''

"This is a small town, Adams,'' the lawman declared. "Ain't many men in this place who'd be much help in a fight. Figure you'd want to take on a gang of hootowls without anybody to back you up?''

"I'm not criticizing how you run your town, Sheriff,'' the Gunsmith assured him. "But if you think I'm going to stand for you arresting me to appease Edward Black, you'd better think again, fella.''

"Just calm down, Adams,'' Greyelk urged. "I reckon I can't arrest you for protecting yourself, but I don't care for your attitude about how I run this town.''

"Maybe I spoke too soon, Sheriff,'' Clint allowed. "I can't blame you if you don't want to tangle with the Black gang. Still, Marcel and I didn't start any trouble. We just had to finish it.''

"Well,'' Greyelk sighed. "I'll throw Sterling outta town. I don't advise you to hang around Piercetown too long, Adams. I wouldn't be a bit surprised if Blackie decides to come lookin' for you. He don't like folks killin' his men.''

"If this *cochon* comes for us,'' Marcel declared proudly, "we will be ready for him.''

FOUR

After Lonny Sterling was escorted from the saloon, and the two dead men were carried out, Clint Adams and Marcel sat at a table with two glasses and a pitcher of beer.

"This has been like old times, eh?" Duboir remarked. "Remember the Lacombe syndicate in New Orleans? Such an adventure we had."

"Marcel," Clint began. "What the hell are you doing in Oklahoma Territory?"

"I decided to leave New Orleans rather abruptly," the Frenchman replied with a shrug.

"In other words you *had* to leave New Orleans."

"It became wise for me to do so," Marcel admitted.

"God," Clint sighed. "How'd it happen?"

"It started with a misunderstanding," Marcel said.

"That means there was a woman involved," the Gunsmith commented. "I sort of figured that."

"She was a real beauty, Clint," the Frenchman smiled.

"Hair as black as a raven's wing and eyes the color of the sky at sunset."

"And she was married too, right?" Clint guessed.

"*Oui,*" Marcel frowned. "Her husband caught us together and drew a gun. I was forced to defend myself. I only wounded him. A minor sword cut to force him to drop the gun. But the idiot suddenly lunged at me before I could move my sword. *C'est dommage.*"

"Sounds like you'd have a hard time convincing a jury what happened," Clint mused.

"I doubt that I would get an opportunity to stand trial," the Frenchman sighed. "The man I killed was a police captain."

"Holy shit," Clint groaned. "When you get into trouble you really dive in with both feet, Marcel."

"I did not plan this to happen, *mon ami,*" Marcel insisted. "But, since it has, I must be about to have a change of luck for it is my great fortune to meet you again, Clint."

"I wouldn't say we've been all that lucky for each other so far," the Gunsmith muttered.

"I disagree," Marcel smiled. "But then you saved my life, *mon ami.*"

"We both saved each other a few times back in New Orleans," Clint recalled. "No sense trying to keep track of who saved who more times than the other."

"*Oui,*" Marcel agreed happily. "I remember the battles we fought back then. The final fight on Lacombe's ship was exciting, no? They still talk of it with respect back in New Orleans. That great brute Jules nearly killed you, but you still managed to defeat him."

26

The Gunsmith remembered Jules. Lacombe's chief enforcer and personal bodyguard, Jules had been a monster of a man. Almost six-and-a-half-feet tall and built like a baby mountain, Jules' right foot had been amputated and replaced with one made of steel. Worse, Jules had also been a *savate* expert which made his steel foot a very deadly weapon indeed.

"Oh, speaking of Jules," Marcel began. "Did you know that hulk managed to escape from the hospital where he had been recovering from that near fatal fall he suffered? He just limped away and no one ever saw him again."

"Wouldn't bet on it," the Gunsmith remarked dryly. "The son of a bitch caught up with me about five months ago."

"*Zut!*" Marcel exclaimed. "Did you kill him this time?"

"Let's just say his limping days are over," Clint replied. "Have you been thinking about what you're going to do out West?"

"First I must adjust to this new environment," Marcel declared with a smile. "And thank God, I have found you. You can help me."

"First thing you'd better do is get some different clothes," the Gunsmith advised. "Dressed up like a fancy dude is bound to get you in trouble."

"*Oui,*" the Frenchman agreed. "And I must also learn how to use a six-gun. What better instructor could I ask for than the Gunsmith?"

"No, Marcel," Clint shook his head. "I'm sorry, but I can't teach you how to quick-draw."

"But why not?" Duboir asked. "Surely, you must realize that a man needs to be able to defend himself. You would not deny me this most basic right would you?"

"Marcel," Clint began. "The last time I taught a fella to shoot was a long time ago. That was back in 1873 at a place called Palmerville, Wyoming. Fella I taught was Marshal Dale Leighton. He'd been shot during a hold up. Leighton caught a bullet in his right arm and the limb had to be amputated. Well, I taught Dale to shoot left-handed. He learned real well. *Too* well."

"What happened?" Marcel inquired.

"Leighton was bitter about the loss of his right arm, and he took it out on everybody else," the Gunsmith recalled. "When he acquired his new prowess as a pistolman, Dale started to like killing people. He gunned down a lot of men before I was finally forced to meet him in the street myself."

"You killed him?"

"I didn't have any choice," Clint replied. "But what matters is the fact I was responsible for teaching Leighton to shoot left-handed. That means I have to accept a certain degree of guilt for the men he killed."

"Nonsense," Marcel scoffed. "If you taught some one to ride a horse and the person fell off and broke his neck, would you blame yourself?"

"I don't know," Clint replied. "But I don't want to teach anyone how to shoot again. Not even you, Marcel."

"You know me well enough to know I am not a bitter cold-blooded killer, *mon ami*," the Frenchman stated. "I do not want a reputation as a gunfighter, and I only want to learn to use a gun for self-defense. Of course, if you refuse to help me, I'll just have to try to learn on my own."

"You'd probably shoot yourself in the foot," the Gunsmith muttered. "All right, Marcel. We'll start tomorrow."

FIVE

The Gunsmith checked into the local hotel. Like everything else in Piercetown, the place didn't have a name. It was just a hotel. Clint hadn't seen many towns as drab as Piercetown. It had all the character and color of a glass of water.

Clint mounted the stairs with his bedroll under one arm and his .45-caliber Springfield carbine slung on a shoulder. He located the room with the same number on its door as the key the desk clerk had given him. The Gunsmith unlocked the door and prepared to enter.

Suddenly, the sixth sense of a survival expert rang an alarm inside Clint's head. He felt the presence of someone waiting for him inside the room. The Gunsmith kicked open the door and dropped to one knee, putting the butt-stock of his Springfield to his shoulder.

"Oh, my Lord!" a female voice gasped.

A young woman stood in the middle of the room. She was tall and shapely with a perfect hourglass figure mounted on long legs. The woman wore a dark-blue cotton dress which accented her shoulder-length blonde hair and nearly matched the color of her velvety eyes.

The Gunsmith was startled to find such a lovely young lady in his room, but he'd known enough treacherous females in the past to be leery nonetheless. Clint rose and approached the woman.

"Maybe we've got a misunderstanding here," Clint began as he lowered the carbine. "But I think this is my room."

"Oh, please don't tell the sheriff," she urged. "I don't want to get in any trouble."

"What are you doing here?" the Gunsmith asked.

"Will you close the door?" she asked. "I don't want anyone to see me."

Clint obliged. He shook his head, puzzled by how things had suddenly started to happen. One right after another.

"My name is Penelope Bayer," the woman explained. "I arrived on the stage today."

"I heard about you," the Gunsmith nodded.

"What?" she blinked with surprise.

"I heard that a very beautiful woman got off the stagecoach today," Clint explained.

"Why, thank you, Mr.—?"

"Just call me Clint," he replied. "Now, tell me how you wound up in this room."

"I picked the lock," she answered sheepishly. "You

see, I don't have enough money to pay for a room here, so I sneaked upstairs while the desk clerk was visiting the outhouse. Then I just used a hairpin and slipped into this room.''

"Well, Penelope—'' Clint began.

"Penny will be fine.''

"Penny, I don't want to get you in any trouble,'' he assured her. "I'll just spread out my bedroll on the floor, and you can have the bed.''

"Certainly not,'' Penny said. "You paid for this room. The bed should be yours.''

"I'm not going to let a lady sleep on the floor while I have a mattress under me,'' the Gunsmith insisted.

"Then we'll have to share the bed,'' Penny announced with a shrug.

"Whatever you say, ma'am,'' Clint replied.

He knew when there was no need to argue with a woman.

Penny turned down the flame of the kerosene lamp and blew it out. Behind the veil of shadows, the woman quickly stripped off her dress and climbed into bed. Clint followed her example. The Gunsmith wasn't quite sure what Penny had in mind, but he didn't feel like going to sleep right away.

He lay beside her on the mattress. The woman leaned close and kissed him on the cheek. Penny's firm, round breasts pressed against his upper arm. Clint turned to her and placed his lips to her mouth.

The woman responded with passion. Her tongue danced inside Clint's mouth. The Gunsmith's hands explored Penny's body, stroking her warm flesh slowly, running his palm along the side of her torso to her breasts.

Clint fondled them and lowered his lips to her nipples. He drew on her gently, teasing the hard nipple with his tongue and teeth. The woman sighed with pleasure as she spread her legs apart as if to offer an invitation to the Gunsmith.

Clint resisted the impulse to accept immediately. He knew the biggest mistake a man can make in bed with a woman is to rush. He continued to stroke and fondle and kiss Penny. His fingers found her soft, sensitive areas. His lips and tongue crept along her neck to the jawline.

"Oh, Clint," Penny gasped.

She slid a hand between Clint's legs and gripped his penis. Penny squeezed the rigid pole of flesh and steered it into the center of her womanhood. The Gunsmith slid himself into the firm, wet pocket of flesh.

Clint worked himself slowly deeper and waited until he felt her body squirm and rise to meet his thrusts. Then he began to lunge faster and harder.

Clint thrust again and again. The woman suddenly gasped and convulsed in a wild orgasm. The Gunsmith slowed his tempo and carefully began to stroke and kiss Penny again. He gently rolled his hips to rotate his throbbing member inside the woman.

Penny began to climb to the zenith once more. This time Clint rode with her. The woman exploded into another quivering orgasm. The Gunsmith joined her. His hot seed burst within her womb. Clint sighed with satisfaction.

"Oh, Clint," she whispered. "I'm glad I picked this room."

"Me too," he replied simply as he embraced the woman gently. "Let's see if we can't make each other glad all over again."

SIX

Marcel Duboir met Clint Adams in the hotel lobby the following morning. The Gunsmith had been surprised when he awoke and discovered Penny had already left. He almost wondered if she had been a dream.

"I visited the general store," Marcel announced as he opened his jacket to reveal a brand-new gunbelt with silver studs in the ornate leather. "What do you think of my selection?"

The Gunsmith couldn't resist a smile. Marcel looked absurd, dressed in his city suit with a white stetson two sizes too large for his head and a fancy gunbelt which looked like it belonged to a bandido chief.

"Belt looks all right," Clint decided. "A little gaudy maybe, but if it works, it'll be fine. Let's see your gun."

"It's a forty-five Colt," the Frenchman declared as he

drew the pistol and handed it to Clint butt-first. "Just like yours."

The pistol had little in common with the Gunsmith's modified double-action revolver. Marcel's Colt looked fine on the outside, but the back plate to the cylinder was pitted and rusty. The trigger arm was worn and inside the barrel looked like a gopher tunnel, complete with rodent shit.

"I'll have to do some work on this goddamn garden tool," Clint remarked. "When I'm sure you can fire this thing without having it blow up in your face, we can see how she shoots."

"Is the gun really that bad?" Marcel frowned.

"The fella who sold this thing to you should have kissed you afterward, Marcel," Clint replied. " 'Cause he sure fucked you with this gun."

"That sounds like it would be most uncomfortable," Marcel laughed. *"C'est la vie,"* the Frenchman replied with a shrug.

After the Gunsmith finished repairing Marcel's Colt, he returned the gun to its new owner and took the Frenchman to the livery stable. Charlie Spotted-Horse had a few animals available for rent, a dollar a day. None of the horses were very impressive, but Charlie had treated them well even if their previous owners had not.

Marcel was hardly an authority on horseflesh so the Gunsmith selected his nag. Clint shook his head when he saw two slump-backed critters that looked as if they'd been used to hauling logs tied to their saddles. Another animal, a piebald gelding was blind in one eye, streaked with the yellows and had mucus coming out its nostrils.

At last he settled for a roan Morgan. The beast was overweight and its teeth were a bit rotted, but it was the only animal which seemed strong enough to support Marcel's weight. The Frenchman paid in advance for the Morgan.

"Charlie," Clint began. "I think you'd better shoot that piebald. Looks awful sick, and he's so old I wouldn't be surprised if he used to be in the calvary during the Revolutionary War."

"He is a very sorry horse," Charlie agreed. "But I can not bring myself to shoot an animal. Not even to ease its suffering."

"Well," Clint began as he strolled over to the piebald. "Personally, I can't stand to think of this poor critter wasting away and maybe making the rest of the horses sick."

Clint suddenly drew his Colt and thrust the muzzle behind the horse's ear. He shot the poor beast, pumping a .45 slug into the piebald's brain. The animal was dead before it hit the ground.

"Marcel and I will bury him," Clint told the startled hostler. "Better tell Sheriff Greyelk what happened before he gets too riled and comes charging over here with that scatter gun of his."

"Who will pay for the horse?" Charlie demanded.

"Marcel will," the Gunsmith volunteered.

"I will?" the Frenchman replied with surprise.

"Sure you will," Clint nodded. "But not more than five dollars. You've already been taken today."

"More than once I think," Marcel muttered as he opened his billfold once more.

It was almost noon before Clint and Marcel finally found a good spot for shooting practice. The Gunsmith selected an area about five miles away from Piercetown. A clearing in the forest with a scrawny creek and a bunch of dead trees, the site was surrounded by an overhang of earth which would absorb bullets instead of causing ricochets.

"All right, Marcel," Clint began as he faced the overhang. "The first thing you do when you're about to practice with a gun is you make sure the area is safe. Don't want to put a bullet in some innocent passerby who picked today to go walking."

"Very well," Marcel replied.

"The second thing you do is make damn sure your horse is tied down good and solid," the Gunsmith continued. "Gunshots will startle the hell out of any animal that hasn't been trained to overcome its natural gun-shyness. Duke is well-trained, but I still tie him down just in case."

"I understand," Marcel nodded.

"Now, we'll shoot at that pile of dead tree branches," Clint decided. "Stuff is brittle so it'll bust apart when a bullet strikes. No ricochet problems. You want to give it a try now?"

"Oh," Marcel blinked, "but of course."

The Frenchman quickly reached for his gun. Marcel had excellent reflexes, but his draw was clumsy. The front sight of his Colt caught on the holster as he jerked the revolver from leather. He snapped his arm out straight, fumbled the hammer to full-cock and pulled the trigger. A bullet slapped dirt from the ground two feet in front of the woodpile.

"Not as easy as it looks," the Gunsmith remarked. "Before you try to use a gun fast, first learn to use it right. You were as clumsy as a virgin on his wedding night, Marcel. You tensed up and that made your motions choppy and awkward. You didn't take time to aim, and you pulled the trigger instead of squeezing it."

"I know," Marcel admitted with a sigh.

"You wouldn't have done that with a dueling pistol," Clint stated. "Now, think of the Colt as a dueling pistol. Take your time and aim it the same way you would a single-shot handgun. Aim carefully and *squeeze* the trigger."

Marcel followed instructions. The second round struck the pile. Splinters of wood hopped from the tree limbs. Clint nodded his approval.

"Before you can draw and shoot," the Gunsmith explained, "you have to know the weapon. Like a sword, it should feel right in your hand. You have to know that weapon. Know how it feels in your fist. Get familiar with the weight and size, the length of the barrel and the width of the grips. You have to get used to the climb of the recoil and the impact through your wrist."

"The front sight caught on my holster," Marcel said. "Perhaps I should file it off."

"Like hell," Clint told him. "Remove the sight and you reduce accuracy. Most gunfights are between opponents less than ten feet apart. You don't need too much accuracy then, you might think. Well, you do if you plan to put a bullet where it'll stop a man. Besides, if a fella manages to get behind some sort of cover, you might not get a large target to shoot at. Accuracy is important. So are the sights to a six-gun."

"I understand," Marcel smiled. "So I practice until the pistol feels like part of my hand."

"That's the idea," the Gunsmith confirmed. "Until your hand doesn't feel right without the gun in it. Just aim and fire. Remember all the rules and repeat them over and over again. Eventually it all becomes second nature."

"Words to live by," Marcel mused.

"To *stay* alive by," the Gunsmith corrected.

SEVEN

Clint Adams and Marcel Duboir remained at the improvised firing range for two hours and then headed back to Piercetown. The stagecoach driver stood beside his vehicle, waiting for the pair to approach. The driver and his partner had spent the night in town, but now they were ready to move on.

"Mister Dew-ball," the driver called to Marcel. "We's fixin' to leave now. Figured you'd be ridin' on to Kansas, sir."

"No, thank you," Marcel replied. "I've come upon an old friend of mine, and I plan to stay in town for a few days."

"Suit yerself, Mister Dew-ball," the driver shrugged.

The Gunsmith saw a lovely and familiar face stare out from the window of the coach. Penny smiled sadly. Clint approached the vehicle and tipped his hat to her.

"I didn't know you'd be moving on so soon," Clint remarked.

"I didn't see any reason to tell you," Penny replied. "I hope you understand."

"Any man who thinks he can understand women is a fool," the Gunsmith smiled. "But I certainly don't have anything to complain about."

"Neither do I," Penny agreed. "And I'd stay a while if I could. My ride is all the way back to Lawrence, Kansas. My folks are waiting for me there and I got to get back home. Spent all my money on this trip, so I can't afford to waste a single day."

"If you need some money—" Clint began.

"I assume you're not trying to be insulting, Clint," the woman replied stiffly. "But I don't need or want charity, and I certainly wouldn't accept money for . . . well, for some other reason either."

"I didn't mean anything," the Gunsmith assured her. "I'm just worried about you. I'd just feel better if I did something to help you."

"Don't worry about me," Penny smiled. "I can take care of myself. You just look after yourself, Clint Adams. If you're ever in Lawrence, we'll get in touch again."

The driver climbed up to the top of the coach. The man riding shotgun cracked open his Stevens side-by-side and checked the shells. The ammunition hadn't gone anywhere since he had last checked the shotgun an hour earlier. The driver gathered up the reins and whipped them across the flanks of his team. The stagecoach rolled forward and headed for the town limits of Piercetown.

"Charming lady, eh?" Marcel commented. "Perhaps

a bit cold, but charming.''

"I wouldn't know," the Gunsmith replied.

"Do you remember what *merde* means, Clint?"

"Sure," Clint nodded. "That was our old password. '*Merde* is French for shit, but shit is just shit in English.' Who could forget something like that.''

"Your reply to my remark about the lady was *merde*, Clint," Marcel told him.

"You sound like you need a drink," the Gunsmith stated. "I know I could use one right now."

They turned and headed for the saloon. Three men stood at the batwings. One jasper was tall and well-built with a broad chest and a lantern jaw which looked like he could use it to knock down a brick wall. The man was dressed entirely in black from the crown of his stetson to the heels of his boots. Even the grips of his revolver were black.

"You must be Clint Adams," the stranger declared.

"Yeah," the Gunsmith admitted. "And I figure you must be Edward Black."

"That's a fact," Black nodded. "Want to tell you somethin', Gunsmith. I know you got a big reputation as a fast gun. They say you're the fastest draw around now that Bill Hickok died.''

"I hear you're pretty fast too, Blackie," Clint replied.

"I do all right," the outlaw leader said. "You and your dude buddy killed two of my boys yesterday. I don't like that, but I reckon they started it. We ain't got no quarrel, Adams. Keep it that way."

"Blackie," Clint sighed, "I understand that you have to show your men you aren't scared of me."

"I ain't scared of you, Adams," Black stated. Clint saw the hardness in the outlaw's eyes and knew Black was telling the truth.

"I didn't say you were," Clint assured him. "And I don't want you to be. Now, I don't see that we have anything to prove to each other, and I'd sure hate for one of us to get killed just to try to prove something to somebody else."

"You don't bother me," Blackie said. "I don't bother you, but if you plan on collecting that one thousand dollars on my head, you'd best change your plans pronto. You savvy?"

"Don't worry about me, Blackie," Clint told him. "There's no need for us to be enemies."

"You ain't exactly on the same side of the law as I am, Adams," Black commented.

"Maybe not," Clint agreed. "But I'm not wearing a badge. Haven't done that for a long time."

"So I've heard, but we ain't on the same side."

"We aren't at war either."

"Not yet," Black smiled thinly. "And you'd best hope that don't happen, Adams. You can't tangle with me and win. Not here anyway."

Edward Black gestured to his men. They followed him as the outlaw leader marched to a trio of horses tied to a rail by the livery. Marcel Duboir uttered a tense sigh of relief.

"I thought there was going to be trouble," the Frenchman said.

"I thought you liked trouble," Clint remarked.

"Not always," Marcel admitted. "And I think Black is the sort of trouble I can live without."

"He's the kind of trouble that can make living goddamn difficult," the Gunsmith stated. "And it won't take too much to set off something with him either."

"What do you think we should do?" Marcel asked.

"Well, are you really in love with this town?"

"Surely you jest," the Frenchman replied. "The most interesting part of this town rode out of here on the stagecoach."

"Then we don't have a real good reason to stay," the Gunsmith decided. "And a couple of reasons to leave."

"Very good reasons to leave," Marcel agreed.

"Then tomorrow morning we'll leave and head for someplace that has more to offer than Piercetown," Clint suggested.

"That's an excellent idea, Clint."

"I come up with some of those from time to time," the Gunsmith replied. "Here's another one: Let's go get those drinks."

EIGHT

The Gunsmith and Marcel Duboir left Piercetown shortly after dawn. The Frenchman sat beside Clint at the driver's seat of the Gunsmith's wagon. Duke was tied to a guideline at the rear of the vehicle. They headed west in the direction of the forest.

"Why are we going this way?" Marcel inquired.

"You want another shooting lesson, don't you?" the Gunsmith replied. "Might take us a while to find another good spot, so I figure we'll use that clearing again. Besides, one direction is as good as another."

"As long as it doesn't lead to New Orleans," Marcel sighed. "God, I miss my city. New Orleans is more than buildings and streets. It is a world unto itself."

"Have you thought about heading for San Francisco?" Clint asked. "I think you'd feel more at home there than any place else west of New Orleans."

"Perhaps," Marcel shrugged. "I've been so busy running the last month or so, I haven't really had time to make any plans. The only goal I've had for a while now has been trying to stay alive and get as far away from New Orleans as possible."

"Well, nobody will be chasing you out here," Clint assured him. "Oklahoma Territory is a regular haven for fugitives and outlaws."

"What fine company we can look forward to," the Frenchman sighed.

"We're almost at the clearing," the Gunsmith announced.

They reached the improvised firing range. Clint and Marcel climbed down from the wagon. The Gunsmith ground hobbled the horses to the wagon team while Marcel scanned the area, looking for innocent passersby.

"Clint!" the Frenchman rasped. "Take a look at those trees and tell me if you see the same thing I see."

Clint obliged. A pale, shapely figure was running through the forest. The shape silently, but swiftly slipped between tree trunks and ducked under low branches. The Gunsmith saw a stream of long, black hair and recognized the delightful mounds at the form's upper torso. Nipples stared back at Clint like two dark eyes.

"Unless we're both having the same mirage," the Gunsmith began, "there's a naked woman headed in our direction."

"I didn't think things like this happened in the West," Marcel commented, gazing at the shapely figure.

"It's happening right now," the Gunsmith told him. The woman suddenly saw the two men and Clint's wagon. Her eyes expanded in horror, and she bolted to the north. Clint glimpsed the woman's bare back. Her hands were tied together at the wrist. Long angry welts streaked her shoulder blades, lower back and the rounded arches of her buttocks.

"Stop, you bitch!" a man's voice bellowed.

His command was followed by the harsh report of a rifle. The Gunsmith and Marcel Duboir saw three men appear from the trees. The trio had on shabby clothes and crumpled hats with shapeless brims. Two men carried rifles while their partner wielded a whip.

"I think we ought to have a talk with these fellas," the Gunsmith whispered.

"How do you want to handle this?" Marcel inquired, reaching for his pistol.

"Back me up," Clint replied. "And don't advertise your position until the shooting starts."

Marcel moved behind a tree as Clint approached the trio. One of the riflemen swung his weapon toward Clint. The Gunsmith's revolver roared before the enemy gunman could fire his weapon. The man's face burst into a crimson pulp, and he slumped to the ground in a trembling, dying lump.

The other rifleman whirled and triggered his Winchester. A bullet splintered bark from a tree above Clint's hurtling form as he dove for the ground. Marcel appeared from his shelter and carefully aimed his revolver.

"Hey, *cochon*!" he snapped as he cocked the pistol.

The gunman turned and Marcel squeezed the trigger. A .45 slug punched into the man's chest, blowing his heart to bits.

The third member of the trio, armed with a bullwhip, hurled the leather cord aside and turned to flee. The Gunsmith lowered the aim of his revolver and fired a bullet through the back of the man's right knee.

The jasper screamed when his bone shattered. He fell forward and struck a tree. The man slumped to the ground. Clint approached the fallen man, his Colt held ready.

"Marcel," he called to his friend. "Try to find the woman. I'll check on these bastards."

"*Oui*," the Frenchman replied. "Take care, *mon ami*."

The Gunsmith only needed to glance down at the first two men to know they were dead. The third man lay at the base of the tree. His head was turned in an awkward position, his chin resting on a shoulder. The man's neck had been broken when he fell against the tree.

"Drop the gun!" a voice snarled.

Clint glanced up, expecting to see the muzzle of a gun staring back at him. But the voice belonged to one of a pair of men who had the drop on Marcel and the woman.

"Shit." The Gunsmith barely breathed the word. He wondered how many more opponents were lurking in the forest.

Marcel's empty hands were raised in surrender as he and the naked woman were escorted at gunpoint by their two captors. Clint slipped behind the tree trunk and waited for them to draw closer.

"We know you're out there somewhere," one of the captors called out. "We got your friend. We'll kill him and the woman unless you throw out your gun and give up."

The man who spoke had a revolver pointed at Marcel's head. His partner held a Henry carbine as he scanned the forest, looking for the Gunsmith. Clint considered the situation. If he startled the hootowls, he could get Marcel killed in the process. A subtle distraction seemed the best bet.

Clint found a small rock and tossed it into a clump of bushes. The rustle of leaves caught the attention of the gunmen. The rifleman whirled and aimed his weapon at the bush. The other man merely glanced in the same direction.

He was distracted for less than a second, but that was all Marcel needed. The Frenchman pivoted and slammed a forearm into the wrist behind the gunman's pistol. The man's revolver fell from his numb fingers. Marcel grabbed his arm in both hands and snapped a lightning-fast *savate* kick to his abdomen.

The rifleman started to turn. Clint snap-aimed and fired his modified Colt. The man dropped his Henry and staggered backward, his left hand clutching at his shattered shoulder.

Marcel kicked his opponent in the gut a second time and then swung his foot high. The heel of his boot crashed into the gunman's jaw. The hootowl collapsed with a moan.

"Well," Marcel said with a sigh of relief. "Today's practice certainly turned out to be an interesting lesson after all."

"I wouldn't mind if things were a little less interesting from time to time," the Gunsmith replied.

NINE

Clint Adams tried to prepare for anything that might happen while he was on the trail so he kept a lot of special supplies in his wagon. Among these included a couple sets of handcuffs and some leg irons. He and Marcel chained the two surviving hootowls in the back of the rig.

"I'm gonna bleed to death," the wounded man rasped, staring at the bloodied bandage strapped to his shoulder.

"Maybe," the Gunsmith replied with a shrug.

"I gotta have a doctor," the man pleaded. "You gotta get me to a doctor."

"Then you'd better hope there's one in Piercetown," Clint told him. "Because that's where we're going."

The Gunsmith climbed into the driver's seat. The woman sat beside him. She held a blanket wrapped around her nakedness. Marcel Duboir sat inside the wagon, a pistol trained on the two captives.

"Well, lady," the Gunsmith began as he gathered up the reins. "Figure you can tell us what's going on now?"

"Might start by telling us your name, my dear," Marcel suggested.

"Eve," the woman began, "Eve Walters. I escaped from Paradise."

"Paradise?" Marcel inquired. "Indeed, you look like an angel, but those whip marks suggest you've been through hell."

"Yeah," the Gunsmith added. "And those fellas we tangled with weren't choirboys."

"Paradise is a small town several miles from here," Eve answered. "At least, they call it a town. It is really a prison. A place where they hold women captive and sell them to whoremasters."

"White slavery?" Marcel asked. "Out here?"

"Why not?" Clint answered. "Lots of outlaws here in Oklahoma Territory. Most of them fled here to avoid the law in other states. Figures that some of those fellas wouldn't be content to just hide out. Sounds like somebody decided to go into the prostitution business to try to make a profit."

"My sister Janis is still back there," Eve said, desperation in her voice. "I can't just leave her there. They're going to sell her to some monster who will take her God knows where and then—"

"Just calm down a bit," the Gunsmith urged. "Now, who are these fellas back in Paradise?"

"The town is run by a man named Thaddeus Harlow," Eve replied. "Most of his men call him Captain Harlow."

"Have you ever heard of this character, Clint?" Marcel inquired.

"Hell," the Gunsmith replied. "I'm not familiar with the criminal career of every son of a bitch west of the Ohio Valley."

"Oh? I thought you'd met most of them."

"Think again, Marcel." Clint turned to Eve. "Tell us about this Harlow."

"He's a vicious brute," Eve explained. "He and his men abduct women and take them to Paradise. Then they beat and rape their prisoners to break down our will. When they feel a woman is no longer strong enough to resist, they sell them to whoretraders."

"Where are these women sent?" the Gunsmith asked.

"I don't know," she replied. "Some are sent to mining towns. Others to harbor whorehouses. I understand some are even sent to Mexico. That's what they told us. I don't know how much of it is true."

"It's possible," Clint remarked. "The further away Harlow can send the women the less apt they'll be to try to escape later."

"What are we going to do, Clint?" Marcel inquired.

"First, we'll talk to Sheriff Greyelk," Clint answered. "We'll see what he can do."

"You don't sound very hopeful," Eve said sadly.

"I'm not counting on much help from Greyelk," the Gunsmith admitted. "He's not really a bad lawman, but he has to consider the safety of his town first. I'm not sure he'll be able to help much, even if he wants to."

"But that shouldn't stop us from taking matters into our own hands," Marcel suggested happily.

"Jesus," Clint muttered. "I knew you'd say something like that."

"What does he mean?" Eve asked.

"He means we'll help you and your sister and whoever else Harlow has locked up in Paradise," the Gunsmith replied. "But we're just not sure how we'll do it yet."

TEN

Sheriff Greyelk listened to their story. Clint, Marcel and Eve stood in the lawman's office and watched him shake his head. They knew the Gunsmith's prediction about Greyelk would prove to be accurate.

"I don't see that I can do much of anything about this," the sheriff sighed. "I know where this Paradise is, more or less, but it's out of my jurisdiction. Figure you'll have to call the federal marshals to handle this."

"Is there a telegraph office in Piercetown?" the Gunsmith asked.

"No," Greyelk answered. "The closest one I know of is at Fort Newburg. That's about three days ride from here."

"Even if we can get the marshals to investigate," Clint began, "it'd take weeks before they could get out here to take action."

"Then we'll have to do this some other way," Marcel commented.

"I don't think I want to hear this," Greyelk said.

"I don't think I do either," Clint sighed. "Look, Sheriff, maybe you can do something for us. The two men we brought in need to be locked up. Can you put them in your jail until other arrangements can be made?"

"No problem," Greyelk agreed. "I'll have Doc Jakes take a look at the wounded man you brought in."

"Good," the Gunsmith nodded. "Well, the sun will be setting in about an hour. I think we'd better get Eve something to eat and a place to stay before we do anything else."

"I suppose Harlow and his Paradise can wait until morning," Marcel agreed. "That'll give us a while to think about how we want to handle this."

"Just the kind of subject I like to sleep on," the Gunsmith muttered.

Clint Adams escorted Eve Walters upstairs to her hotel room. Clad in a brand new gingham dress she looked fresh and relaxed. Clint figured she was really more exhausted by her ordeal, but a hot bath and a good meal had done wonders for her nonetheless.

"Janis and I were traveling down from Kansas with our father and brother," she remarked. "Mother had died during childbirth the year before. Pa decided we all needed a new start somewhere else where Ma wouldn't haunt everything we saw. So we headed for Oklahoma. Harlow's men attacked our wagon. They killed Pa and my brother. Then they took Janis and me—"

"I don't think you should talk about this right now," the Gunsmith urged. "You've been through a lot. Better rest, Eve. Don't worry about your sister. We'll take care of her."

"I don't know what you and Marcel can do alone against Harlow and his cutthroats," Eve sighed. "He has more than twenty men working for him. Every one of them is a murderous beast."

"Well," Clint shrugged. "He lost five fellas already. That's not a bad start."

"You've been very good to me, Clint," the young woman smiled. "I can never repay you for such kindness."

"You don't owe me anything," he assured her as he inserted the key in the door and unlocked it. "Just get some sleep and trust us. Marcel and I have taken on worse odds in the past and won. Have a little faith."

"Clint," she began awkwardly. "Could you do me a favor?"

"Name it," he replied.

"The doctor gave me a balm cream for my back," Eve explained. "Would you put it on for me?"

"Well, sure," Clint replied, surprised by her request.

They entered the room. Eve did not bother to light the lamp. She stripped off her dress. Clint saw the pale, shapely outline of her lovely young body amid the shadows. He swallowed hard, telling himself not to get any wrong ideas about an innocent young lady who had already suffered a great deal at the hands of many men.

Eve lay on her belly across the bed. The Gunsmith opened a jar of balm and sat beside her. He scooped out some cream and ran his hand over her scarred back. His hand rubbed the ointment into her shoulder blades and lower back. He hesitated a moment before applying the cream to her buttocks.

"You have a nice touch, Clint," the woman declared, almost purring with pleasure.

"Thanks," he replied because he didn't know what else to say.

"Are you and Marcel really going to head for Paradise tomorrow?" she asked.

"That's the plan," the Gunsmith answered.

"You're both willing to risk your lives for people you don't even know," she said. "Why?"

"Reckon we're just made that way, Eve," Clint replied. "I think it would be too much to say either Marcel or I are exactly heroes like in the storybooks, but we're not the sort of fellas who could just walk away from something like this and live with ourselves afterward."

"But you might be killed," Eve whispered.

"A fella can get killed under any sort of circumstances," the Gunsmith replied. "Hell, I could fall off my horse and break my neck or get hit by a bolt of lightning. No point worrying about that."

"I've heard that sex between a man and woman can be wonderful," Eve remarked. "Is that so?"

"Yes," Clint assured her. "I know you've had some bad experiences with men, but not all of us are vicious bastards like Harlow and his crew. Rape is nothing like making love. It's like comparing a bitter cold blizzard to a cool breeze on a summer night."

"Will you make love to me?" the woman asked softly.

"Eve," the Gunsmith began. "You're not obliged to—"

"I don't ask you for your sake," she told him. "I want you tonight because you might not return to me. I don't want to spend the rest of my life wondering what it may have been like with you, Clint."

The Gunsmith unbuttoned his shirt and tossed it aside. He scooped Eve up in his arms and crushed his mouth against hers. His tongue caressed the edges of her teeth and probed deeper into her mouth. His hands gently stroked her shoulders and back, slowly traveling along the velvet surface of her skin.

"Oh, Clint," the woman sighed.

He removed his boots and trousers. Clint hung his gunbelt on the headboard within easy reach in case of an emergency. Then he sat naked beside her. His hands continued to explore Eve's body as he kissed her neck, running the tip of his tongue along the hollow of her throat.

They sprawled across the mattress. Clint was mindful of her injured back. He had once been whipped by El Espectro's bandido gang in Mexico so he appreciated the pain caused by a lash.* Eve climbed on top of Clint and reached between his legs to fondle his swollen manhood.

The Gunsmith arched his back to kiss her breasts. His mouth closed on a nipple and drew on it gently. His tongue ran small circles around its growing firmness. The woman moaned with pleasure and guided Clint's hard member into her womb.

*The Gunsmith #19: Bandido Blood

She closed around his penis like a warm satin fist. Clint ground his buttocks against the mattress, working himself inside her. Eve crooned happily and began to rock to and fro, joyfully impaled upon Clint's manhood.

Eve gradually rode up and down the length of his cock. She increased the tempo until her body hopped up and down on his crotch. Then she cried out as an orgasm swept through her like an electric shock.

Yet she wanted more. Eve pumped again, faster and faster until Clint could no longer contain himself: He was reaching the limit fast. The Gunsmith urgently thrust himself inside her. His seed escaped, and he groaned with pleasure although he feared he had failed to satisfy the woman's needs.

However, Eve also gasped as her second orgasm exploded. She convulsed and thrashed on top of Clint, yanking and twisting his penis with each motion.

"Sweet Jesus," she whispered. "That was wonderful. I understand now."

"It's one of the best things in life," Clint assured her as he leaned forward to kiss Eve. "But there are a lot of other good things waiting for you too. Give yourself some time, and they'll come your way."

"You know what?" Eve smiled. "I'm beginning to believe that."

"Have I ever lied to you?" he grinned back at her.

ELEVEN

"Next time," Marcel Duboir complained as he rode the paunchy old Morgan alongside the Gunsmith, mounted on his magnificent black Arabian, "I'll take the woman up to her room."

"Why don't we drop the subject?" Clint inquired as he glanced about the grassy meadows which flanked the dirt road.

"I know what you and Eve did last night, *mon ami*," the Frenchman muttered. "My room is right next to hers and the walls are very thin in case you didn't notice."

"Did you listen with a glass pressed against the wall," the Gunsmith asked in an annoyed tone. "Or did you drill a hole so you could peek in and watch?"

"Neither one," Marcel replied. "I put a pillow over my head and tried to block it out."

"I appreciate your respect for my privacy," Clint said

dryly. "Now, where the hell is Paradise? Sheriff Greyelk was sure this road would lead to Harlow's town."

"It must be farther away than he realized," the Frenchman shrugged. "I wish we had come up with a different plan. The more I think about the one we decided to use, the more I can see how it might go wrong."

"Don't think about that," Clint urged. "There's some risk involved, but not too much considering the only other ideas we could come up with were a lot more dangerous."

"Well, we'll soon see just how well our plan works," Marcel announced as they saw a collection of shabby little buildings in the distance.

"That's Paradise?" the Gunsmith snorted. "Hell, it looks even worse than Piercetown."

"Oh, I'm sure it is much worse," the Frenchman remarked.

Paradise consisted of a group of ugly little shacks and a larger structure which resembled a poorly built barn. Several men squatted around a campfire scraping up beans from tin plates and shoveling the food in their mouths. Two figures armed with rifles stepped forward to confront Clint and Marcel.

"Morning," Clint called to the sentries. "This must be Paradise."

"That's what we reckon," one of the guards replied. "Now what do you fellas want here?"

Several other gunhawks joined the two sentries. Clint recognized the breed. They were bottom-of-the-barrel hired help with guns. They were the type of stupid brutes who would always be willing pawns for any son of a bitch who could offer them a dishonest way of making a living.

"We want to talk business," Clint answered. "Where's Captain Harlow?"

"Who wants to know?" a gravel-laced voice demanded.

The others stepped aside to make a path for a large man dressed in dark trousers and a threadbare jacket with tarnished brass buttons. A sea captain's cap was perched on his shaggy head. He scratched at the fleas inside his thick, rust-colored beard as he stared up at the Gunsmith and Marcel Duboir.

"Captain Harlow?" the Gunsmith asked.

"You answer me first, mate," the shaggy man insisted, a trace of London in his accent. "Who the 'ell are you?"

"My name is Marcel Lacombe," the Frenchman lied. "Perhaps you've heard of the Lacombes of New Orleans."

"I 'eard of Gaston Lacombe who run a bloody great organization awhile back," the Briton nodded. "But I 'ear they ain't much now. Gaston got hisself 'anged along with most of his mates."

"That's correct," Marcel replied. "Gaston was my uncle. The syndicate he created is dead, but I still have to make a dollar, *oui*?"

"That ain't me problem," the Briton shrugged. "And I ain't interested unless you can tell me some way your problem concerns me business."

"I've opened a couple brothels near Galveston," Marcel answered. "And I need some women to work there."

"You need some sluts, eh?" the Englishman laughed. "Too bad you ain't around your fellow frogs. Plenty of sluts then."

Several of the gunmen chuckled. Marcel took the remark in stride. Clint quietly scanned over the town, trying to log details about Paradise in his memory.

"You don't like the French, sir?" Marcel asked.

"Show me an Englishman that likes frogs, and I'll show you a bloomin' idiot," the bearded man replied gruffly. "But I won't let that get in the way of doin' business—if you can meet me price, Lacombe."

"I take it you're Captain Harlow," Marcel remarked.

"I'm Harlow," the Briton confirmed. "And you'll address me as either Captain or Sir. Understand?"

"If that's what you want, Captain," Marcel nodded.

"Now who's the chap with you," Harlow inquired. "Ain't said much, but he looks like a gunfighter to me."

"I'm sort of a bodyguard," the Gunsmith replied. "Mr. Lacombe isn't familiar with this territory, so I'm acting as sort of guide and protector."

"Reckon you'd have much of a chance against all me mates, Mr. Bodyguard?" Harlow chuckled.

"Maybe not," Clint shrugged. "But I reckon I'd put my first bullet in your head just to make sure I wouldn't die alone. How's that sound, Captain?"

Marcel stiffened in his saddle. Several of Harlow's men tensed. Others backed away in case they needed to run for cover in a hurry. Harlow merely stared at the Gunsmith. Clint didn't bat an eye as he displayed his best professional poker face.

"Sounds like you've got balls of brass, mate," Harlow smiled. "Got a name to go with them?"

"Call me Clint," the Gunsmith replied.

"Jesus H. Christ," one of the henchman gasped. "It's Clint Adams!"

"That's a fact," Clint nodded.

"And who the bleedin' 'ell is Clint Adams?" Harlow asked his men.

"They call him the Gunsmith, sir," one of the gunhands replied. "They say he's the fastest gun in the whole goddamn world."

"I thought Blackie was supposed to be the best," Harlow remarked. "That's what all you chaps keep tellin' me."

"Blackie is the fastest gun in the Oklahoma Territory," a tall, beanpole-thin man confirmed. "At least he was until the Gunsmith arrived."

"Well," Harlow smiled. "Lacombe must be payin' you quite a lot, Adams."

"Enough," the Gunsmith replied. "I don't work cheap. This isn't the sort of thing I usually do for a living, so I have to get a good salary to accept this sort of a job."

"Might consider workin' for me," Harlow mused.

"I'm moving on after this is over," Clint told him. "Have to go to Galveston with Mr. Lacombe. After I get him home, safe and sound, he'll pay me my salary. Two thousand dollars."

Harlow whistled softly. "That is a pretty penny, mate."

"The cost of the best is never cheap," Marcel declared. "I hope you noticed that Clint mentioned the fact my money is back in Galveston. If any of you are thinking about trying to rob us, that would be a waste of time."

"And a fatal mistake for at least three or four of you," Clint added. "I figure I can shoot that many before you can kill me."

None of Harlow's henchmen seemed to doubt this for a minute.

"Hold on, mates," Harlow began. "We'd best get an understandin' here, Mr. Lacombe. I don't care if this Clint Adams fella is the fastest gunman in the bleedin' universe, that still doesn't change how I do business. No credit, mate. You pay cold, hard cash for me women; or you'll have to look elsewhere for your sluts."

"But you're a businessman, aren't you?" Clint asked. "A long term business agreement is worth more than a one-time deal for a couple women."

"Are you Lacombe's business manager as well as his gunman, Adams?" Harlow inquired.

"I'm just trying to look after his best interests," Clint answered simply.

"Really?" Harlow cocked his head to one side. "Let's talk about business. What kind of a deal can we make, Lacombe?"

"I'll arrange for an agent to come out here to pay for four or more women at a time."

"How often?" Harlow inquired.

"Four times a year. Once every three months."

"So you'll buy your first women three months from now?" Harlow shook his head. "That's a bit of a delay."

"You want me to buy some women now?" Marcel raised his eyebrows. "I'm not really prepared to take any back with me."

"Just one or two, mate," the Briton replied.

"I didn't bring much money."

"You don't trust me?" Harlow inquired.

"No Frenchman trusts the English."

"*Touché*, Lacombe," Harlow laughed. "All right. I

70

have to admit business has been a bit slow this month. I've got too many women right now. Some whoremasters from a mining camp or two got some last month, and we sold some others to some 'alf-breeds headed for Mexico. That was last month, and they won't be back for quite a while. We can use some more cash, mate."

"How much?" Clint asked.

"For each woman?" Harlow scratched his filthy beard. "Let's say three hundred each."

"Let's show the captain our good faith, Mr. Lacombe," the Gunsmith suggested. "You asked me to hold onto four hundred for you. Why don't we offer him two hundred a woman?"

"That sounds reasonable," Marcel replied with a wooden nod, astonished by Clint's suggestion.

"You're askin' me to sell these women for a hundred dollars less?" Harlow shook his head. "That's not how I do business, mate."

"Look, Captain," Clint forced a smile. "You just admitted that things are slow. That means you either sell some women now, or you hold them until a new customer opens up. I know how you people operate. White slavers gang rape and beat a woman until she's lost all her willpower to resist. If you have to hold them for another month you'll be lucky if all your females aren't dead or crippled up pretty bad."

"Two hundred and seventy-five," Harlow declared.

"Maybe we should just buy one woman," Marcel shrugged, still wondering what the hell Clint was up to.

"Two hundred and fifty," Harlow announced. "And not a bleedin' penny less. That's less than a hundred pounds in real money, for crissake."

"Come to think of it," the Gunsmith grinned, "Mr. Lacombe gave me five hundred dollars to look after for him."

"You bloody horsetrader," Harlow smiled. "Well, we got a deal then?"

"Ask Mr. Lacombe," Clint replied.

"I guess so," the Frenchman answered, bewildered by the incident.

"Then come along and make your selection, gents," Harlow invited.

TWELVE

Captain Harlow led Clint Adams and Marcel Duboir to the barn. A fat man with a bullwhip draped over his shoulders like a pet snake, sat on a crate near the entrance. Harlow told the sentry to open the door.

The fat man obeyed. He drew back a heavy bolt and seized the door handle. The sound of flesh striking flesh was followed by a low groan as the henchman doubled up. A pair of small hands clasped together and chopped the fat man in the nape of the neck. He fell to one knee.

A naked woman with blonde hair reached for the pistol on the dazed man's hip. She glanced up long enough for Clint to see her face and recognize the woman.

She was Penelope Bayer.

"Bloody 'ell," Harlow snarled.

Before Penny could draw the sentry's pistol, Harlow stepped forward and swung his fist. Clint's stomach knotted when he heard the impact of knuckles against Penny's jaw. The woman dropped senseless to the floor of the barn.

"You idiot!" Harlow snarled as he grabbed the fat man by the back of his collar and hauled him out of the barn. "Gettin' bested by a bleedin' bitch like that. Oughta shoot you meself."

"Where is she?" the sentry spat, rubbing his genitals with one hand as he unslung the whip from his neck. "I'll whip her tits off for kickin' me in my balls."

The Gunsmith struggled to control his rage. He wanted to kill every one of Harlow's men, but he realized any rash action would be suicide for himself and Marcel. Yet, he could not stand by and allow Penny to be flogged by these scum.

Clint stepped forward and swept a forearm under the fat man's chin. The stroke lifted the man off the ground and then dumped him on his back hard. The henchman glared at Clint and tried to get ample leverage to use his whip. Marcel stamped a boot on the lash, pinning the whip to the ground.

"We don't want our property disfigured," the Gunsmith growled.

"You're throwin' your weight around a bit too much, Adams," Harlow snapped. "Discipline is my business here."

"We don't want to pay good money for scarred females, Captain," Clint insisted. "Letting this son of a bitch flog the women isn't going to make them more attractive. After all, would you pay for a woman who looked like she got caught under a moving wagon?"

"I wouldn't pay period," Harlow spat. "Neither

would none of my lads. We get to screw so many women it's a ruddy bore.''

"Can we take a look at the merchandise now, Captain Harlow?" Marcel inquired.

Harlow led Clint and Marcel across the threshold of the barn. The interior was filthy. The floor was covered by a carpet of dirty straw. Five naked women were huddled in a corner. Their flesh was marred by an assortment of bruises and scars. Frightened eyes gazed up at the men.

Penny Bayer still lay unconscious in the middle of the floor. A trickle of blood formed a wet ribbon at the corner of her mouth and an ugly dark bruise discolored the side of her jaw. The Gunsmith looked down at her, grateful to see she was still alive.

"This is one spirited lady," he declared, trying to sound amused. "Good body on her too."

"I don't advise you to take that one," Harlow warned. "She's the newest addition 'ere. Ain't broken in yet. This bitch will be more apt to try to escape than any of the others."

"I think we can handle her," Marcel shrugged. "Clint seems to fancy her."

"Watch your balls, lad," Harlow chuckled. "But then yours are made of brass anyway."

"Then she'll just break a toe if she kicks me there," the Gunsmith said dryly. "See anything you like, Mr. Lacombe?"

"I believe I'll take the one with red hair," Marcel replied as he seized one of the women and pulled her to her feet.

The woman cringed fearfully, ducking her head as if

fearful of being struck. Marcel had to play his role to the hilt. He roughly shoved the woman toward the door.

"Stand over there and be quiet, *mon cheri*," the Frenchman growled. "Or I'll put my boot up your pretty little ass."

"I'll take my money now," Harlow demanded.

"You have any clothes for these two?" the Gunsmith asked as he handed the Briton five hundred dollars. "Riding around with a couple naked women is apt to attract a lot of unwanted attention."

"We got some clothes for 'em, don't worry 'bout that, mate," Harlow replied. "Now, I reckon that takes care of our business for a while."

"For three months or so," Marcel confirmed.

"Come back anytime, mate," Harlow smiled. "We always got some females for sale around here."

"Oh, don't worry," the Gunsmith grinned. "We'll be back."

THIRTEEN

"I nearly had a heart attack back there," Marcel Duboir admitted as he and Clint Adams rode from the town of Paradise.

"And here I thought you were having a good time," the Gunsmith remarked as he glanced over his shoulder to see if any of Harlow's people had decided to follow them.

Penny Bayer and the red-haired woman rode a mule which Harlow had generously supplied along with the purchase. Penny was still unconscious and draped across the neck of the animal.

"Why did you give your real name to those bastards, Clint?" Marcel asked. "Wasn't that inviting trouble?"

"I didn't see what it could hurt," the Gunsmith replied. "Besides, with so many hootowls on Harlow's payroll, I half-expected Edward Black's gang to be part of the crowd. If I tried to pretend to be somebody else that would have made Black suspicious as hell."

"Harlow mentioned Blackie," Marcel recalled. "It sounded to me like he's familiar with Black too."

"Yeah," Clint agreed. "But Black's gang wasn't there and Black damn sure wasn't. Too many people we're insisting that I'm quicker on the draw than Black. He would have felt it would be necessary to come out and challenge me to a contest if he had heard that."

"Would you have accepted?" Marcel asked.

The Gunsmith nodded. "Nobody would have listened to us if we appeared to be cowards. Around trash like that you either act tough, or they eat you alive."

"I wondered why you were being so blunt back there," the Frenchman remarked. "Although, I was beginning to catch on."

"I noticed," Clint said. "You did just fine, Marcel."

"For a man who nearly had a heart attack," Marcel nodded. "But I don't understand why anyone familiar with your reputation would believe you'd be a gunman bodyguard for a white slaver. Everyone familiar with the legend of the Gunsmith—"

"Please," Clint muttered. "That expression makes me feel like puking."

"Like it or not," the Frenchman shrugged, "it is still true. And anyone familiar with your legend knows you aren't a criminal."

"But outlaws think *everyone* is a criminal," Clint explained. "Corrupt people can't think of anybody being less corrupt than themselves."

"We would have been in a hell of a mess if any of those scum had remembered hearing or reading that you helped to crush Lacombe's syndicate in New Orleans," Marcel remarked. "How would you explain riding with 'Marcel Lacombe.' Now that makes *me* ill. Imagine, being forced to claim I was related to that bastard!"

"I know it was hard on you, Marcel," Clint smiled. "But it's over now. As for anybody recalling that I helped to put Gaston Lacombe out of business, we could have just told them I was working for you even then. You were trying to capture control of your uncle's syndicate, but the police ruined your scheme."

"You scared me when you agreed to pay Harlow five hundred dollars for those two ladies," the Frenchman admitted. "I didn't even know you had that much money with you."

"Well, I figured Harlow might insist on a down payment of some kind," Clint said. "Figured I'd bring some cash along just in case."

"They might have decided to just kill us and take the money anyway."

"That's what you call a calculated risk," Clint told him. "Part of gambling."

"A part I can live without," Marcel commented. "Is there any other reason you wanted to pay Harlow for two of his female prisoners?"

"Well," the Gunsmith began, "if our plans don't quite work out, I figured we might at least free two women."

"You mean if we get killed," the Frenchman said.

Clint nodded. "If that happens, it'll mean things didn't quite work out."

"*Merde,*" Marcel sighed. "And you think *I'm* the reckless one!"

"I'm a gambler," Clint stated. "So I'll take risks

sometimes, even if it means pushing against the odds. But you can be plum crazy sometimes, Marcel.''

''*Oui*,'' the Frenchman was forced to agree.

''I think we're far enough from Harlow's Paradise,'' the Gunsmith decided. ''Let's stop and let the ladies know they're not really on their way to a brothel.''

''I think Penny is recovering consciousness,'' Marcel commented.

''That pig Harlow,'' Clint rasped. ''He punched her pretty hard. It's a wonder he didn't break her jaw.''

''One more score for us to settle with that *cochon*,'' Marcel agreed.

Clint and his friend brought their horses to a halt and dismounted. The red-haired woman stiffened with fear as the pair approached. Penny Bayer, still slung over the neck of the mule, turned her head and looked up at the Gunsmith.

''Clint?'' she asked, afraid she might be dreaming.

''That's right, Penny,'' the Gunsmith assured her as he helped her off the mule. ''You're going to be alright now. Everything will be all right.''

''Where am I?'' she glanced about at the surrounding forest. ''That awful place—''

''No longer threatens you,'' Marcel declared, helping the redhead down from the mule. ''*Either* of you. For we are your liberators, not your jailers. *Oui*?''

The redhead spat in Marcel's face.

''You want to sample the merchandise?'' she sneered. ''Save your oily charm 'cause I'm not impressed. You can starve us, beat us up and rape us, but don't expect us to listen to your lies and submit. I'll be damned if I'll make it fun for you—''

"The rescue business isn't what it used to be," Marcel sighed, wiping the saliva from his face.

"Lady, will you just shut up and let us explain what's going on?" Clint demanded. "Yesterday Marcel and I were in the forest a few miles east of here. A young woman named Eve Walters suddenly appeared, followed by five gunmen."

"Eve?" the redhead stared at Clint. "Where is she? Eve is my sister."

"Then you must be Janis," the Gunsmith said. "Eve told us you were still a prisoner in Harlow's Paradise."

"Please," Janis pleaded, "where is Eve? Is she alright?"

"She's fine," Clint assured the redhead. "We took her to Piercetown and she's got a nice, cozy room in the hotel."

"Did you kill the bastards who were trying to catch her?" Janis asked, obviously hoping for a positive answer.

"Three of them," Marcel replied. "The other two are securely locked in Sheriff Greyelk's jail. I imagine they're both in considerable pain since Clint shot one of them, and I personally kicked in the other man's teeth."

"Oh, I wish I'd seen that," Janis admitted.

"You might get to later," Marcel smiled. "Kicking in villains' teeth is sort of a specialty of mine."

"What about the other women who are still prisoners in Paradise?" Penny asked.

"Marcel and I plan to slip into Harlow's town after dark to free the other women," Clint explained.

"There are too many of those scum back there," Penny declared. "You'll both get killed for sure."

"We already discussed that possibility," Marcel commented, "and we decided not to include it as part of our plan."

FOURTEEN

They rode a couple more miles before setting up camp. Clint Adams took some supplies from his saddle bags and prepared some sour dough biscuits, beans, jerky and coffee. Penny rubbed her sore jaw as she ate, but there was nothing wrong with her appetite.

"You two ladies can ride the mule to Piercetown," the Gunsmith instructed. "Just follow the road and it'll lead you right to safety."

"I thought I was safe in the stagecoach too," Penny remarked, "until those animals attacked it in broad daylight. They murdered the driver and the man riding shotgun and took me to that awful place."

"She's right," Janis added. "Harlow and his pack prey on the roads. We'd be safer to just stay here until you get back."

"There's a possibility we might not come back," Clint warned.

"I think you will," Penny replied. "I'm willing to wait here too. If you're not back by dawn we'll move on to Piercetown."

"Well," Marcel began as he drew his cane sword from its wooden sheath. "Even if Harlow's men combed the area looking for accomplices, I doubt that they'd look this far from Paradise."

"Not until sunrise," the Gunsmith agreed. "But I still think you ladies should move on to Piercetown now."

"We'll be alright," Penny assured him. "But can we have a gun just in case?"

"I'll leave my Springfield carbine with you," Clint nodded. "Know how to use it?"

"Sure," she answered.

"How much can you two tell me about how they handle security in Paradise?" Clint asked. "Where sentries patrol the area, and how many are on duty after dark?"

"In case you didn't notice," Janis began. "There aren't any windows in that barn we were kept in. We couldn't really see anything that went on outside."

"Well, at least we got a good look at Harlow's set up," Marcel shrugged. "Not very complicated. There seemed to be about fifteen men there. I figure that means no less than two guards on duty and not more than four."

"Figure between four and six," the Gunsmith corrected. "Don't forget that they lost five of their men recently. Five fellas chase after a runaway woman with her hands tied behind her back. None of them ever come back."

"I overheard a guard say that some of the men think those men must have encountered an Indian forest devil which is supposed to be half-animal and half-man," Janis commented with amusement.

"A sasquatch," Clint commented. He wasn't amused. The Gunsmith knew the sasquatch was more than a legend.

"That means they never found the bodies of the three men we killed," Marcel mused. "They must not have looked very hard because we didn't bother to bury the bastards."

"They'll still have more guards on duty," Clint insisted. "I take it they always have someone stationed at the door of the barn."

"That's right," Janis confirmed.

"If you're right, Clint," Marcel began, "that means we'll have to take care of between five to seven of the bastards. That's almost half of Harlow's men."

Janis watched the Frenchman sharpen the long steel blade of his sword with a whetstone. He slid the sword back into his cane and twisted the handle to secure it in place.

"Are you really going to use that thing?" she asked.

"But of course," Marcel replied cheerfully. "It is more silent than a gun, and I've used it many times before. Eh, Clint?"

"Marcel is an expert with a sword," the Gunsmith agreed. "He knows what he's doing."

Clint reached into his saddlebag and removed a bowie knife in a leather sheath. He drew the weapon and examined the blade to be certain it was still sharp. He hadn't honed the edge for a while, but then he hadn't used the knife either. Clint didn't care for a knife as a weapon.

"Is that what you intend to use on sentries?" the Frenchman inquired.

"I'll try," Clint said without much conviction. "I suggest we try to get some rest between now and sunset. We got one hell of a night ahead of us."

FIFTEEN

The Gunsmith stretched out under the shade of an elm tree and placed his stetson over his face. He soon drifted into a shallow level of sleep which would allow his body and mind to rest while his senses and reflexes remained alert to danger.

Soldiers on the battlefield learn to sleep in this manner. Although the Gunsmith had never been a military man, he had lived with danger and the constant threat of deadly assault virtually all his adult life. His right hand rested on the butt of the Colt revolver on his hip as he slept.

The rustle of bushes interrupted his slumber. Clint remained motionless, his breath steady. He appeared to be sound asleep as he listened to the unfamiliar sounds, trying to determine if they were a preamble to danger.

He heard whispers. A man and a woman. More bushes rustled. The woman sighed with passion. Clint heard bodies moving against the ground, close to the foot-high grass a couple of hundred yards from where he lay.

Footfalls contributed to the background of sounds. The tread of someone who weighed little and walked softly approached. Clint heard the rustle of cloth against cloth. The folds of a skirt, he guessed.

The Gunsmith raised a thumb to the brim of his stetson and cocked back his hat from his eyes. Penny Bayer walked toward him.

"I didn't mean to wake you up, Clint," she whispered.

"You didn't," he assured her.

The lovely woman sat down beside him. Clint slid an arm around her shoulders. Penny placed her head against his chest, and Clint stroked her hair gently.

"Janis decided to apologize to Marcel for spitting in his face earlier today," Penny explained.

"Sounds like they're getting along all right now," the Gunsmith mused.

"I think so too," Penny replied. "How about us?"

"As I recall," Clint began as he cupped her face in his hands and gazed into her eyes, "we got along pretty well before."

Their mouths met. Flesh pressed together hard. Tongues wiggled and probed. Clint pulled her closer. The woman slipped her fingers inside his shirt and ran her hand along the carpet of hair on his chest. She unbuttoned the shirt and slid her fingers down his torso.

Penny felt the rigid pole of his manhood straining the fabric of his trousers. She sat up and unfastened his trousers to free his swollen penis. The woman smiled as she stroked the stiff length of his hard shaft.

She leaned forward and kissed the head of his penis. Her tongue moved around the circumference of his manhood. Her lips traveled down the length of his cock to the root. Penny licked him gently as her mouth slowly traveled back to the head.

Penny's lips slipped over the top. She drew on him tenderly. Her mouth moved along the shaft once more. His member throbbed within the warm, damp cavern as she gradually rode up and down.

Her head moved faster. Clint felt himself near the brink. He whispered Penny's name to warn her, but the woman paid no heed and continued to pump his cock inside her mouth.

At last, Clint had no endurance left. His member erupted like a miniature volcano. Penny accepted this without complaint. She milked his member with her lips, drawing all his seed into her mouth.

"That was terrific," Clint whispered to Penny.

Clint embraced her and continued to stroke and fondle her. He gradually unhooked the back of her dress and peeled off her clothes. They undressed each other until both were totally naked beneath the elm tree.

Clint assumed the dominant role. His hands glided over Penny's flesh, caressing her breasts and belly. He ran his fingers along her hips and eased them to Penny's inner thigh. She purred as he massaged her womb.

The Gunsmith's maleness had swollen once more. Penny stroked his member as Clint skillfully eased his fingers into her wetness. The woman parted her legs wide to receive him.

"I'm ready, Clint," Penny whispered softly.

He mounted her. The woman eagerly led his hard penis between her thighs and opened the lips of her vagina to welcome him. Clint slid his manhood into the warm sheath of flesh. He entered her slowly, working the woman up to a peak of pleasure she had never known before.

Penny exploded in a trembling orgasm. Clint's member was still rigid. He drove himself harder and faster. Penny gasped as a second orgasm tumbled behind the first.

"Oh, God," Penny gasped.

Clint continued to pump himself inside her. The woman raked her fingernails across his back as her body bucked and thrashed in yet another climax. This time Clint rode to glory with her, and he emptied himself within her love chamber.

The couple lay pleasantly exhausted, a sheen of perspiration on their naked flesh like morning dew. The Gunsmith could remember few occasions when a woman had given him such pleasure. Of course, he knew the reason.

If the raid on Paradise failed, it might well be the last time.

SIXTEEN

A scattering of stars twinkled in the night sky like a handful of tiny diamonds. The quarter moon dominated the firmament like a great sliver of light amid the velvet universe above. However, the Gunsmith and Marcel Duboir did not take time to enjoy the natural beauty of the Oklahoma sky as they stealthily approached the town of Paradise.

A sentry strolled from the edge of the town limits and walked to a tree trunk. He propped his rifle against the tree and unbuttoned his trousers. Following whatever instinct motivates men to piss at the base of a tree trunk, he freed his penis and began to urinate.

Sharp, pointed steel pressed against his backbone. The guard gasped in terror as the point poked harder between his shoulder blades.

"Raise your hands, or I'll pin you to the tree like a

butterfly on a collector's display board," Marcel whispered the warning.

The guard's hands slowly rose. Clint Adams stepped beside the frightened sentry. The man's eyes widened with fear when he saw moonlight flash on the blade the Gunsmith drew from his belt sheath.

Clint's arm dove low. The sentry uttered a breathless moan of dumbfounded terror. The Gunsmith had placed the razor edge of his bowie knife a fraction of an inch from the root of the sentry's penis.

"We don't have all night, fella," Clint rasped. "You either cooperate and answer our questions, or you'll be less of a man for it. If you don't think I'm serious, call my bluff, you bastard. It'd be a goddamn pleasure to use this knife on scum like you."

"Oh, shit," the man whimpered. "I'll talk."

"How many guards on duty tonight?" Clint demanded.

"Four includin' me," the hootowl answered. "Oh, and Willard is guardin' the barn where we keep the women."

"How do you people patrol the town?" Clint asked. "Do the guards march a set pattern around the place, or do they basically just sit and watch."

"We walk patrols," the guard replied. "The Captain likes us to do things sort of military like. Of course, Willard just sits there by the door of the barn. Only one way in and one way outta that thing."

"If I find out you're lying," Clint warned, "I'll come back and chop off everything you've got between your legs."

"I ain't lyin', mister," the man assured him.

"We'll find out," the Gunsmith stated.

He suddenly grabbed the guard's hair with both hands and bashed the fellow's forehead into the tree. Clint repeated the tactic and rammed the man's skull against the trunk again. The Gunsmith released his victim and allowed the outlaw to slump to the ground, senseless.

"You sounded as if you really intended to use that knife," Marcel whispered.

"I'm not sure whether I would have or not," Clint confessed as he knelt by the unconscious sentry and quickly bound the man's hands behind his back.

"Should we take care of the roving guards first?" Marcel inquired. "Then the *cochon* at the barn?"

"Yeah," Clint confirmed as he tied the unconscious man's ankles together and gagged him. "We'd better get to work before anybody notices this fella is taking a hell of a long time to spring a leak."

"*Oui,*" the Frenchman nodded. "Good luck and good hunting, *mon ami.*"

The Gunsmith and Marcel found two more sentries patrolling the perimeter of the town. Clint gestured toward one of the guards and placed a thumb to his own chest. Marcel nodded. The Gunsmith crept after his chosen target, leaving the other sentry for Marcel to deal with.

Clint drew his knife. His stomach knotted. Clint envied Marcel's confidence with a blade. The knife felt awkward in his fist as he slithered up behind the sentry.

The Gunsmith didn't want to use the knife. The guard's back remained turned toward Clint. The Gunsmith clenched his teeth and prepared to attack. He hesitated. The man turned and stared at the Gunsmith's face.

Clint lunged with the knife, but his attack was clumsy.

The sentry swung his rifle. The barrel chopped Clint's bowie knife from his hand. The guard prepared to follow up with a butt-stroke at Clint's head.

The Gunsmith charged and both men toppled to the ground. Clint landed on top of the sentry and seized the man's rifle. The outlaw struggled to keep possession of his weapon. The man opened his mouth to cry for help, but Clint quickly lashed a fist to the side of his jaw.

The guard groaned and twisted the rifle, trying to knock the Gunsmith off his chest. Clint grabbed the frame of the long gun and shoved with all his might. He put all his weight behind the move and jammed the barrel of the rifle across the outlaw's throat.

An ugly choking gurgle escaped from the sentry's crushed throat. Clint continued to apply pressure, pressing the bar of the rifle harder across the man's windpipe as his body convulsed frantically.

The convulsions ceased. The Gunsmith climbed to his feet and unsteadily stepped over the man's corpse. That had been close, he thought. Too close.

He glanced over at the second guard's position. Marcel Duboir stood over the sentry's corpse, calmly wiping blood off the sword with the dead man's bandanna. Marcel and Clint exchanged nods and slipped back into the shadows to begin stalking the other sentries.

The Gunsmith reached the back of the barn and cautiously advanced along the side of the building. He froze when he saw the last of the roving patrol sentries march past a column of shacks. The guard walked to a campfire and poured himself a cup of coffee from a blue tin pot. Clint waited for him to move on.

Suddenly a cloud slipped across the face of the moon, casting a shadow on the ground near the sentry. The man tossed down his coffee cup, startled by the unexpected movement. He glanced about suspiciously, his rifle braced against a hip.

"Hey, Willard," the guard called to the man stationed in front of the barn.

"What the hell is botherin' you, Link," Willard replied gruffly.

"Somethin's wrong," the guard insisted. "I don't see none of the others walkin' around. Do you?"

"Hell," Willard snorted. "You can't see 'em most of the time anyway. You worry too much."

"And you don't worry enough," Link said. "Captain told us to wake him if anything happened."

"You reckon you gettin' the willies is the sort of thing he meant?" Willard scoffed.

"I figure with five of our men missin' we got a right to the willies," Link answered. "I'm gonna get the Captain."

"Shit," Willard muttered.

A shadow appeared behind Link. A flash of silver sliced through the side of the sentry's neck. The guard dropped his rifle and fell to the ground, both hands clutching the bloodied wound in his neck. Marcel Duboir flicked his wrist to shake some blood from the blade of his sword.

"What the hell—" Willard exclaimed.

Clint Adams dashed around the corner to confront the guard at the entrance of the barn. Willard was a squat, bearded man with tiny pig-eyes and a doorknob-shaped nose. He held a bullwhip in his right fist, but he was about to transfer it to his left hand in order to reach for his sidearm.

The Gunsmith leaped forward like a pouncing puma, his knife held in an overhand grip. He collided with the outlaw before Willard could use his whip or draw his pistol. Clint was familiar with bullwhips and knew a lash is ineffective against an opponent who is extremely close.

His bowie struck deep into the man's upper chest, above the heart and lungs. Willard shrieked as both men landed on the ground. The blade was stuck. Clint couldn't pry it free to try again.

Willard screamed again. The Gunsmith clubbed him across the side of the face with his fist. The guard groaned. Clint hit him again, and the man slumped unconscious.

"We're in trouble, *mon ami*," Marcel announced as he slid his cane sword into its wooden scabbard.

"You noticed," the Gunsmith replied, drawing his modified Colt revolver.

SEVENTEEN

Outlaws poured out of the shacks. Clint and Marcel were stunned by the number of enemy gunmen. There were more than twice as many opponents than the pair had expected.

The Gunsmith aimed his double-action six-gun with both hands and opened fire. His modified Colt blazed with Gatling-gun speed. Four shots cracked so rapidly the echoes tumbled into one another. Three outlaws cried out and collapsed.

Marcel ran to Clint's position. He hastily fired three rounds at the enemy gunmen as he dashed for cover. The Gunsmith yanked back the bolt to the barn door and slipped inside. The Frenchman literally dived head-first across the threshold, pistol in one hand and his cane sword in the other.

Bullets splintered the walls of the barn. Clint ducked low and began to remove the spent cartridge casings from his revolver to replace them with fresh ammunition. Four women cowered in a corner, naked and helpless.

"Good evening, ladies," Marcel declared. "We came to rescue you, but it appears that will be a bit more difficult than we realized."

"What do you mean?" one of the women asked. "Who are you?"

"Introductions will have to wait," Clint replied. "We can't stay here. This barn is a tomb. They can box us up in here until we run out of ammunition or until they get pissed enough to set fire to the barn."

"*Merde*," Marcel muttered.

"This building is made of wood," Clint replied. "If we can get a couple boards loose and pry them from the wall, we can slither through the hole."

"We've tried that," a woman cried hopelessly. "It's no use. We're all going to die here!"

"Shut up, Cindy," a tall dark-haired woman snapped. "We found a couple boards which seemed sort of rotten at the base. We've been trying to work them loose, but we haven't had much—"

A volley of enemy gunfire interrupted her sentence. Several bullets pierced wood and hissed through the interior of the building. Clint stayed low until the shooting eased to a less frantic level.

"My God," Cindy's voice gasped. "You have a gun. Why don't you shoot back?"

"That's what they want," Clint replied as he crawled toward the others. "If I expose myself they'll blast me. Now, where are those rotten boards?"

The dark-haired woman showed them the area. Marcel

knelt by the floor and examined the wood. He then got on his back and aimed both feet at the wall. The Frenchman delivered several powerful *savate* kicks, slamming the heels of his boots into the wood.

A loud crack rewarded his efforts. Marcel drew his cane sword, inserted the point into a gap in the wood, and began to apply pressure against it. The board bulged, then broke loose.

A figure with a rifle suddenly appeared at the entrance. The Gunsmith's Colt roared. The gunman's head recoiled as a .45 slug sliced through it. He crumbled lifeless to the ground.

"Hurry up, Marcel," Clint rasped.

"Do you want me to break my sword?" the Frenchman asked as he worked the blade against the second board.

"Just hurry," the Gunsmith urged.

The Frenchman continued to pry with the blade until the second board finally broke from the wall. The women cried out with joy. Cindy desperately crawled to the hole.

"We're free!" she cried. "We're finally free!"

"Wait," Clint warned.

The woman stuck her head through the gap and wiggled through the hole. The others heard the sound of a hard object striking something solid, followed by a liquid gurgle. Cindy's legs were dragged through the opening.

"Bastards," the Gunsmith snarled. "Everybody move from that wall."

He aimed his Colt at the wall above the hole and fired three double-action rounds through the wood, placing one bullet to the right of the gap, one to the left and the last round directly above it. A scream revealed one of the bullets had struck the outlaw lurking on the other side of the wall.

"You could have hit Cindy!" a woman cried.

"Somebody already did," the Gunsmith declared. "I've heard that sound before. Cindy's skull was cracked open. She's dead."

Two sticks with flaming rags attached to them were hurled inside the barn. The straw on the floor was immediately ignited by the blaze. Fire burst inside the building and spread rapidly.

"We're going to burn!" a woman exclaimed as she rushed forward to try to throw the torches back outside.

Rifle bullets slammed into her. The multiple, large caliber slugs hurled her body into a wall. She fell lifeless, landing face first in the heart of the blaze. Flames crackled in her hair. The stench of charred flesh assaulted the nostrils of the survivors.

Smoke filled the barn rapidly. Clint and the others lay low, unable to move to the entrance or the hole in the opposite wall because the enemy gunmen continued to bombard the barn with a constant salvo of bullets.

The Gunsmith could barely see or breath in the dense smoke. He recalled that most people who die in fires are killed by asphyxiation. This seemed better than burning to death, yet Clint Adams didn't intend to simply lie down and die.

He rose to his feet and tried to aim the pistol toward the entrance. His smoke-filled lungs caused him severe, stabbing pain. Yet he staggered forward, blinking watery eyes to try to clear his vision.

A tall, black figure appeared among the clouds of

smoke. The Gunsmith's arm felt as if it had lead weights strapped to every muscle. He couldn't raise his Colt.

The world suddenly spun. Clint Adams felt himself drift into limbo. He did not feel the impact when his back hit the floor. The smoke seemed to close in around him like the coils of an enormous serpent. He almost welcomed the cold blackness of oblivion.

EIGHTEEN

Consciousness returned with a vengeance. The Gunsmith awoke from the dreams of nothingness, coughing violently. Clint's chin struck his chest. Water and mucus poured from his nostrils.

He vomited on his shirt front. Air entered his nostrils and filled his empty lungs. He spat again and warily raised his head.

"There you go, Adams," a voice chuckled. "You ain't gonna die on us after all."

The Gunsmith opened his eyes to see a blurry, dark figure. He blinked and his vision cleared. The man before him wore black clothes and a stetson. He smiled at Clint as he tilted a canteen to pour water in his cupped palm.

"You damn near died, Adams," Edward Black commented as he tossed the handful of water in Clint's face. "If'n we hadn't drug you outta that barn you'd be burnt up just like that gal. Awful what happened to her, ain't it?''

The Gunsmith didn't reply. The fuzziness inside his head slowly melted away. He realized he was seated in a chair with his hands tied behind his back. Glancing about, he discovered he was inside a filthy one-room shack. Captain Harlow and several others were present. Marcel Duboir was tied to another chair. He appeared to be in the same condition as the Gunsmith—miserable.

''Well, Adams,'' Black sighed as he put the cap on his canteen. ''You made a lot of people unhappy with you tonight.''

Without warning, Black swung the canteen and slammed it across Clint's face. The Gunsmith's head recoiled. The room swam in a blur of dull colors. The salty taste of blood mixed with the sour puke in his mouth.

''Bloody 'ell, Blackie,'' Harlow snapped. ''Don't knock 'im unconscious again. We want'a have a few words with this Gunsmith chap and his frog buddy.''

''The . . . women?'' Clint croaked. His throat felt as if he had gargled with hot sand.

''Two of 'em is dead,'' Harlow replied. ''The other two will be all right after a while. They're feelin' pretty much the same as you are, I suspect.''

''Gotta hand it to you, Adams,'' Black chuckled. ''You sure did a lot of damage for one night's work. Yessir, you and your peacock friend killed eight men, includin' two of my boys, and you got those two gals killed two. We also had to burn down the barn, and I reckon that's your fault as well.''

"You're—" Clint began, but his throat hurt too badly to speak.

"Give the lad some whiskey," Harlow told one of his henchmen. "Use a cup. We don't want any puke on the neck of the bottle."

An outlaw obeyed the order. The liquor was fiery and coarse in Clint's throat, but the taste killed the foul flavor and burned life inside his belly. The Gunsmith looked up at Edward Black.

"You were going to say something to me, Adams?" the outlaw boss inquired.

"You're a yellow-bellied son of a bitch, Black," Clint declared.

Black's fist smashed into the side of Clint's jaw. The Gunsmith groaned. He shook his head to clear it. Black seized Clint's hair and yanked his head back.

"You want to apologize for that remark, Adams?" the outlaw demanded.

"Let's shoot it out, Black," the Gunsmith said. "You know I'm faster than you. You don't have the guts to face me on even terms."

Black's fist struck again.

Clint went unconscious once more.

The Gunsmith awoke, nearly choking on the whiskey which had been poured down his throat. Clint gazed up at a large black man with a drooping mustache and a shaven head. His eyes resembled two black marbles as he stared back at Clint.

"Is he awake, Simba?" Harlow's voice inquired.

"Yes, Captain," the black man replied. He folded his

thickly muscled arms on his chest. "Should I start torture now, sir?"

"Not just yet, Simba," Harlow said as he stepped forward and looked down at Clint. "You're not eager for that sort of questionin', are you mate?"

"Hardly," the Gunsmith confirmed.

"Clint," Marcel called softly. "Are you all right, *mon ami*?"

"That's a goddamn dumb question, Marcel," Clint muttered.

"You two shut mouth," Simba snapped. "Captain want you talk, you talk. Shut mouth 'til then."

"Simba is an old friend of mine," Harlow explained. "He was a Bantu warrior back in Africa, but some bloody idiot made a slave of him. You don't make slaves out of Bantu, eh Simba?"

"Laota, slaves," the African spat with contempt. "Bantu, warrior."

"I bought Simba from a nigger slaver off the Ivory Coast when I still had me ship," Harlow explained. "But I didn't keep 'im in chains for long. Not when I learned Simba was a Bantu. We used to hunt whales awhile back. Simba is the best bloody harpoon thrower you ever laid eyes on."

"How did you go from selling whale blubber to white slavery?" the Gunsmith inquired.

"That's a long, sad story," Harlow sighed. "Me ship got wrecked off the Gulf of Mexico. Most of me men were killed. The rest stuck with me for a while, until they got work with other ships in Galveston. Well, I been captain too long to go back to being a swabby, so I kept lookin' for a new trade. See, tradin' has always been me life. Now, you don't have much in the United States that a man can trade these days. No jewels to speak of, no ivory, you don't even have nigger slaves anymore."

Clint looked at Simba to see his reaction to the Briton's remark. Simba didn't seem to mind at all. Apparently, the Bantu didn't object to black slavery as long as his tribe in general and himself in particular were not included.

"So," Harlow continued. "I eventually hit upon sellin' women. Always a market for that, don't you know. Oklahoma seemed like the best spot for me to do business since the law doesn't seem to care much what we do here. Then *you* have to come along and cause trouble."

"Don't expect an apology," Clint muttered.

"I'm surprised you're so stupid, Adams," Harlow remarked. "Comin' here to try to rescue those bitches was bloody foolhardy. That stunt with Black was just as stupid. You really think I'd let you have a gun even if Black had agreed to a gunfight with you?"

"You got Blackie on a leash?" the Gunsmith asked.

"One he can't see or feel," Harlow nodded. "See, he's sort of hit on hard times since he can't go about robbin' banks and what not for a while. So we're kind of partners right now. Of course, it's my business, so that means I'm the one what's really in charge."

"Does Blackie realize this?" Clint asked dryly.

"That's not your problem, Adams," the Briton told him. "So don't worry about it. Right now, you'd best be concerned with your own troubles, mate."

"Since Marcel and I are still alive," Clint began, "I'm sure you want to tell us about them."

"You took two of my women earlier today," Harlow commented. "Obviously part of your silly rescue scheme. I reckon you probably took that other one too. The little bitch what run away yesterday. Reckon you killed my men too."

"Well," the Gunsmith shrugged, "we're not very likely to do that again—at least not now."

"No bad-mouth Captain," Simba snapped. "Bad-mouth, and I break bone."

The black man picked up a stool and held it upside down. Simba gripped a leg in each fist and ripped the stool apart.

"Break bone like this, Yankee trash-shit," Simba growled.

"Easy, Simba," Harlow urged. "Just relax. I'll tell you when I want you to start aworkin' on these two."

The Bantu nodded and stepped back. He folded his arms on his chest once more and stood as still as a cigar store Indian.

"Simba gets a bit impatient at times," Harlow remarked. "He'd bloody well enjoy torturin' you two. He's good at that gruesome stuff. Practices on small animals when he can't get his hands on people."

"Sometimes I find dedication hard to admire," the Gunsmith commented.

"You'll find it a bloody nightmare if I let Simba have a go at you, mate," the Briton warned. "Of course, you can save yourself a lot of pain and suffering by simply telling me where those women are."

"Did you check all our pockets?" the Gunsmith inquired.

"You're decision, mate," Harlow shrugged. "But believe me, you're going to regret it."

NINETEEN

An explosion startled everyone in the room. Clint Adams flinched from the unexpected sound. Captain Harlow ducked and stared up at the ceiling as if he expected it to cave in. Marcel Duboir muttered something in French which wasn't in Clint's limited vocabulary of the language, but he had a pretty good idea what it probably meant.

Simba had dropped to the floor and covered his head. "Cannon, Captain!" he cried. "Yankee trash-shit use cannon on us! Pray Jesus-God, cannon no hit us!"

"What the bloody hell is—" Harlow began.

Another explosion interrupted the Briton.

"Trash-shit kill us, Captain," Simba declared. "We have no cannon, Captain. What we do so trash-shit no kill us?"

Harlow hurried to a corner and gathered up a gunbelt with a Tranter revolver in a hip holster and a saber hooked to the other side. He buckled the belt around his thick waist and drew the sword.

"All right, Adams," Harlow growled as he thrust the point of the long, thick blade in front of Clint's face. "Tell me what's going on, or I'll cut your eyes out!"

"Your town is being blown to pieces, Captain," the Gunsmith replied.

"You must like the idea of wearing an eye patch, Adams," the Briton hissed. "Because you're going to need two of them."

"Gouge me and this little Paradise of yours will be a pile of toothpicks, Harlow," Clint replied, trying to sound as if he knew what the hell was happening.

"You mean you can stop them?" Harlow demanded.

"Not if I'm tied to this chair," the Gunsmith insisted.

Clint had a hidden "ace up his sleeve"—or rather, under his shirt. His hold-out gun, a diminutive .22-caliber New Line Colt he wore in his belt, under his shirt, had not been discovered by his captors. If he could draw the weapon, Clint might be able to turn the tables.

"You expect me to release you?" Harlow smiled. "You must take me for an idiot."

"You've got a gun and a sword and Simba for protection," the Gunsmith said. "You also had a whole roomful of gunmen before you threw Blackie out of here for using my head for a punching bag. Call them back inside if it'll make you feel safer."

Another explosion erupted outside. Harlow cursed under his breath and slid the saber into its scabbard.

"Simba," he ordered. "Untie Adams."

"Yes, Captain," the Bantu nodded.

Harlow drew his Tranter and aimed it at Clint as Simba

moved behind the Gunsmith and fumbled with the ropes at Clint's wrists. The British outlaw drew closer and thrust the muzzle of his pistol in Clint's face.

"Get up slowly, Adams," he warned. "No tricks, or I'll happily blow your brains out."

Clint's hands were free. He raised them to shoulder level and slowly rose. Simba's breath bombarded the back of his right ear.

"Oh, God!" Marcel cried. "Look at that!"

Harlow and Simba were distracted by the Frenchman's unexpected cry of alarm. The Gunsmith instantly took advantage of this. His left hand shot out and grabbed the Tranter, jamming a finger between the hammer and firing pin.

Clint bent his right elbow and thrust it backward, driving the point into Simba's mouth. The big African yelped and staggered backward, more surprised than hurt.

Harlow pulled the trigger of his Tranter. The hammer snapped down and pinched Clint's finger, which prevented it from striking the firing pin. The Gunsmith's right fist slammed into the Briton's nose, breaking cartilage on impact. Blood spurted from Harlow's nostrils.

Clint rammed a knee between Harlow's legs. The Briton gasped in agony. The Gunsmith grabbed the lapel of Harlow's jacket and swung him around as Simba lunged forward.

The Bantu crashed into his captain. The Gunsmith jumped back and allowed both men to fall to the floor. The Tranter slipped from his finger and landed beside them.

Clint quickly drew his .22 New Line Colt and kicked the Tranter across the floor. Simba started to rise, but froze when he saw the pistol in Clint's fist.

"Captain!" he yelled, staring into the muzzle of the tiny gun.

"Where the 'ell did you 'ave that thing 'idden?" Harlow asked, facing the Gunsmith's belly gun. "Those bloody idiots were supposed to 'ave searched you. Bleedin' shit'eads."

"Shut up and crawl over to that wall," Clint ordered. "Then sit with your backs against the wall and your hands on top of your heads until I tell you to do otherwise."

The pair obliged. Clint moved behind Marcel. Keeping the New Line trained on Harlow and Simba, the Gunsmith clawed at Marcel's bonds with his left hand.

"Thanks for the distraction, friend," Clint told the Frenchman. "I knew you hadn't gone to sleep."

An explosion blasted the door off its hinges. Smoke and dust billowed into the room. Captain Harlow half-ran, half-crawled to the gap. Clint snapped off a hasty shot at the retreating figure. Harlow howled in pain, but he kept moving across the threshold outside.

Simba began to rise, but Clint swung his pistol to cover the big man. The Bantu slumped onto his backside and kept his hands on his head.

"Clint?" Marcel sighed. "Who the hell is setting off those damn explosions?"

"I don't know," the Gunsmith muttered. "What I want to know is whose side are they on?"

TWENTY

Clint Adams finished untying Marcel's wrists. The Frenchman crossed the room and gathered up Harlow's discarded Tranter revolver. He nearly bumped into a small cluttered table. Marcel glanced down at it and recognized two familiar objects among the rubble.

"How considerate," he said with a smile. "They left our gunbelts here."

"Thank God for careless enemies," the Gunsmith said as Marcel handed him his gunbelt.

"My cane sword isn't here," the Frenchman frowned.

"Maybe we'll find it later," Clint said, buckling the gunbelt around his lean waist. "I wonder if that was the last explosion."

Another ear-bashing, spine-rattling blast answered the Gunsmith's speculation.

"Guess not," he muttered.

Clint heard rifles and pistols being fired outside the shack. The Gunsmith suspected the shooting had accompanied the explosions since they began, but he hadn't noticed it until now. Several voices, distorted by the echoes of explosions and gunshots, shouted unintelligible words which still contained a trace of desperation.

"Shall we see what's going on out there?" Marcel inquired, replacing the spent cartridges in his revolver.

"Not much reason to stay here," Clint replied.

"What about him?" the Frenchman gestured toward Simba who still sat on the floor with his hands on his head.

"Not much point in taking him with us," Clint replied as he finished reloading his double-action Colt and put the .22 New Line back inside his shirt. "We might have been able to use Harlow to negotiate a deal with, but I doubt if it would work with Simba for a hostage."

"We can't just leave him here either," the Frenchman stated.

"Tie him up first," the Gunsmith suggested.

"But he's so strong he might break the ropes," Marcel warned.

"The only other choice we have is to shoot him," Clint shrugged.

"Simba no can break rope," the Bantu said quickly, eyes bulging from his ebony features. "Tie Simba and me stay here."

"Do yourself a favor and shut up," Clint told him. He turned to Marcel. "Look, Simba probably deserves a bullet. But it's not exactly self-defense to kill him while he's sitting on his ass without a weapon."

"I suppose I don't like the idea either," Marcel admitted. "All right, *mon ami*. We'll tie him up. I just hope we don't regret it later."

They bound Simba as securely as possible and moved to the remnants of the door. Dust and smoke formed a grimy fog, but they could still see bodies strewn across the ground. Figures darted about amid the haze. Clint and Marcel held their fire until they could be certain of their targets.

"Clint," Marcel whispered, "look there."

The Frenchman pointed at a pair of shapes which advanced from the side of another shed. Although blurred by the dust cloud, both forms appeared to have long hair and slightly bell-shaped lower bodies. Women in skirts.

"Must be Penny and Janis," the Gunsmith mused. "Looks like they're both packing rifles too."

"They're setting off explosives?" Marcel shook his head with disbelief. "Where did they find it, and how would two women know how to use dynamite or blackpowder bombs?"

"We'll ask them," Clint said. "Have to get them to shelter anyway. If we can see them, Harlow's people may be able to see them too."

"Better be careful," Marcel remarked. "I'd hate to be mistaken for an outlaw and wind up getting shot by one of our lady friends."

The two men moved outside, and cautiously approaching the women, called out to Penny and Janis. The women turned. One waved her rifle to acknowledge the fact she recognized the men.

Ironically, the dust and smoke began to settle. Clint and Marcel had not needed to take the risk of announcing their presence on a battlefield. The women could see them clearly in the moonlight.

However, it appeared the danger was over. Half-a-dozen dead outlaws littered the ground, but not a single living opponent was on his feet.

The serpents had been driven out of Paradise.

TWENTY-ONE

"We won!" a man's voice cried at the edge of the outlaw town. "God Almighty, I can hardly believe it! We whupped 'em good and proper!"

Clint Adams was surprised when two familiar figures emerged from the treeline and strolled into Paradise. Sheriff Greyelk and Charlie Spotted-Horse approached the Gunsmith. Both men carried rifles. Charlie also had a gunnysack slung over his shoulder.

"I didn't expect to see you two out here," Clint admitted. "But I'm sure glad you showed up."

"Got to thinkin' about what Harlow was doin' and decided I didn't like the idea much," Greyelk shrugged. "Figured I ought to do somethin' about it whether Paradise happened to be in my jurisdiction or not."

"Sheriff ain't here as a lawman," Charlie added, grinning as he pulled the gunnysack from his shoulder. "Left his badge back in Piercetown, didn't you, Sheriff?"

"This ain't an official trip," Greyelk replied. "No need to drag the town into this."

"These gentlemen were heading toward Paradise," Penny explained. "Janis and I almost took a shot at them because we were afraid they were part of Harlow's crew."

"Yeah," Greyelk nodded. "Of course, Charlie and me figured the gals must've come from Paradise. Lucky for us Clint told them about Eve being at Piercetown. The ladies lowered their guns when we explained that. After seein' how well they can shoot, I'm glad they did."

"What about the explosions?" Marcel asked.

"Well," Greyelk began. "I didn't want to take on a whole gang of bandits all by myself, so I asked Charlie to come along. He used to be a powder-monkey a few years ago. Best dynamite man I know."

"Hell," Charlie shrugged. "Wasn't very hard. Just planted some charges at different spots surroundin' the town and set 'em off. Then I tossed a couple sticks of dynamite into the bastards when they come runnin' out."

"I noticed," the Gunsmith remarked.

Shredded corpses covered the ground. Severed limbs had been hurled several yards from the ragged stumps of mutilated torsos. The stench of blood assaulted their nostrils.

Janis had been unable to endure the grisly scene. She had fallen to her knees and vomited on the grass. None of the others blamed her.

"I don't see Harlow among this mess," Marcel commented. "Of course, I'm not so sure I'd recognize him."

"I haven't noticed Black among the dead either," Clint added. "We'd better assume they both managed to survive."

"If they did," Charlie chuckled, "then they hauled outta here quick with the rest of them yellow-bellies."

"That's what worries me," Clint confessed. "Those two are leaders. The others might simply scatter and run, but Harlow and Black will regroup and plan a new strategy. They're not about to let us get away with screwing up their master plan."

"Reckon we'd better not stand 'round here pattin' ourselves on the back," Sheriff Greyelk remarked.

"Let's make a quick search of the town first," the Gunsmith advised. "Some of the outlaws might be hiding inside the shacks waiting for a chance to ambush us as we start to leave. I'd rather face a man from the front than find out about him after he's put a bullet in my back."

"If we hang around here we might get ambushed by the fellas what run off," Greyelk warned, "if you're right about them regroupin' for attack, Clint."

"Gotta risk it," Clint insisted. "An enemy lying in wait right here is a more serious and immediate threat than one which might be licking its wounds, figuring out how to hit us. Besides, some of the other women might still be alive."

"Let's get amovin'," Charlie Spotted-Horse urged.

"Sheriff," Clint began, "you and Charlie stay together and watch for trouble from outside the camp. Marcel, you and Janis check out half the shacks while Penny and I check the others."

Everyone agreed to the Gunsmith's plan. Clint and Penny approached a shack. The woman covered Clint as he cautiously approached the door and kicked it open without exposing himself to the doorway. His precautions proved to be unnecessary. The shack was empty.

Penny and Clint moved to another shack. The Gunsmith repeated his method of opening the door. He peered inside to see a scrawny, rat-faced man cowered in a corner, a knife clenched in his fist. Clint trained his pistol on the outlaw, quickly scanning the interior of the shack for any others who might be lurking there.

He glanced down at the floor. A bullet of ice seemed to burst from his brain and travel down his spine. Clint's stomach crumbled and an abrupt constriction seized the Gunsmith's throat.

He had found the other women.

Both women lay on the filthy floor of the shack. Still naked, their bodies were covered with bruises and knife cuts. Long, deep gashes in their throats had unleashed twin rivers of blood.

Their lifeless unblinking eyes stared up at Clint, revealing pain and horror, pleading for some sort of justice—or revenge.

The Gunsmith obliged.

"No," the rat-faced outlaw whimpered, when he saw the cold, deadly rage in Clint's expression. "Please—"

Clint ignored the man's pleas as he gazed at the blood-stained knife in the killer's fist. The Gunsmith lowered the aim of his revolver and squeezed the trigger.

The outlaw cried out in agony, as he fell to the floor, clutching at his bloodied crotch. The Gunsmith had castrated him with a well-placed bullet.

"Oh, my God," Penny gasped. Then she saw the mutilated bodies of the two women. "No, it can't be—"

She buried her face in her hands and wept. Clint put an arm around her and led her from the shack. The outlaw continued to howl in torment.

"You can't leave me like this!" he cried out. "Finish me off. Please—"

"You've got a knife," Clint snapped. "Use it."

TWENTY-TWO

Marcel Duboir was in good spirits. He had found his cane sword amid the rubble of the burned barn. The wooden scabbard had been destroyed by the blaze, but the brass handled sword of Toledo steel had survived.

The Frenchman's pleasure was immediately terminated when Clint told him about the other women. Janis burst into tears and buried her face in Marcel's chest. The women had shared a terrible ordeal in Paradise. Four of their friends had died in Harlow's sordid hellhole.

The Gunsmith felt their grief and also experienced a degree of guilt. He had failed to rescue the four women he had returned to Paradise to save. Although he and Marcel had survived, Clint could find no satisfaction in their "victory."

True, Harlow had been driven from his evil town. About a dozen of the outlaw's henchmen were dead, and the town of Paradise was a shambles. Yet the Gunsmith considered the battle a stalemate.

But the night wasn't over yet.

"Sheriff," Clint began, "you and Charlie escort the women out of here and take them to Piercetown. Marcel, you may want to go with them."

"What are you planning to do, *mon ami*?" the Frenchman asked as he slid the tarnished sword into his belt.

"I figure Harlow and his troops will come after us," the Gunsmith explained. "That means they'll either try to hunt us down at night or wait a couple hours for dawn."

"Their horses scattered when the dynamite started to liven things up," Charlie Spotted-Horse stated. "Reckon they'll play hell tryin' to round up their critters, 'specially at night."

"They can't ride at night anyway," Clint commented. "Riding a horse in the dark would be suicide in a forest with low-hanging branches and tree roots jutting out of the ground. If they ride after us, they'll wait until sun up, but they just might try tracking us on foot."

"And what are we going to do about that?" Marcel inquired.

"The others will go ahead, and we'll follow some distance behind them," the Gunsmith explained. "If the bastards pursue, we'll slow them down."

"I trust that means we'll kill them?"

"Nobody is slower than a dead man," the Gunsmith confirmed.

"No, Clint," Penny urged. "It's too dangerous."

"Marcel and I have done this sort of thing before," Clint assured her. "We'll be all right, but we'll be able to work better on our own without having to worry about the rest of you folks.''

"I can't say I like that plan much, Clint," Sheriff Greyelk remarked. "But I reckon nobody has a better one to offer."

"Then it's agreed," Clint nodded. "Charlie, do you have any dynamite left?"

"Four or five sticks," the hostler answered.

"That'll be enough to destroy the shacks here," Clint declared. "Let's not leave Harlow a single building in one piece."

"That'll be a pleasure," Charlie replied with a grin.

The hostler prepared the dynamite, placed the sticks strategically between the remaining shacks and lit the fuses. Charlie joined the others and they hurried out of Paradise to the treeline. Two minutes later, a series of explosions roared as if in a single blast.

The remaining shacks were torn to pieces by the dynamite. Chunks of shattered wood flew in all directions. Dust billowed and filled what used to be the town of Paradise. A coal-oil furnace landed in the center of town, draped in flames.

"Oh, shit!" the Gunsmith exclaimed. "We forgot about Simba. We just blew the bastard to Kingdom Come."

"No such luck, *mon ami*," Marcel replied. "I checked the shack where he was tied up. Simba was gone. I didn't think those ropes would hold him. The African must have slipped out the window while we were talking."

"I just hope he didn't get out of town before Charlie blew up Paradise," Sheriff Greyelk remarked. "If the son of a bitch was part of Harlow's gang he deserves to get his innards spread all over Oklahoma.''

"Maybe," Clint sighed. "I still can't feel as antagonistic toward Simba as I do for the others. After all, Harlow bought him and used Simba, pretending to be the fella's liberator and friend. Seems natural for him to feel loyalty toward the Captain.''

"None of which makes him any less dangerous to us,'' Marcel commented.

"Yeah," the Gunsmith agreed. "I figure he'll be just as eager to kill us as the rest of Harlow's crew. All right, you folks better get moving.''

"Take care, Clint," Penny urged. "We'll meet you back at Piercetown.''

"Good luck," Greyelk said simply as he led Charlie, Penny and Janis into the forest.

"Well, Clint," Marcel began as he watched the others melt into the darkness. "How long do you think it will be before Harlow's gang comes after us?''

"I don't know," the Gunsmith answered. "But I'm more concerned with *how* they're going to do it.''

TWENTY-THREE

The Gunsmith reached for his turnip-shaped pocket watch, then remembered that it and his billfold had been stolen while he was Harlow's prisoner. Clint gazed up at the sky and tried to determine the time by the stars and the color of the sky. A ceiling of tree branches blocked his view.

"Figure we've waited about half-an-hour," he whispered to Marcel Duboir.

"Seems longer," the Frenchman replied.

"Half-an-hour is still more than enough time for Harlow's people to start tracking us," Clint remarked. "Of course, tracking at night is almost impossible. Even an experienced tracker would have a hell of a hard time trying to read signs in the dark."

"Then they're going to wait until sunrise to come after us," Marcel mused.

"Looks that way—" the Gunsmith began, but he abruptly ended the sentence and cocked his head as if listening for something in the night.

"What—" the Frenchman asked.

Clint held up a hand for silence.

Marcel listened, but heard nothing but the wind uttering a low whistle as it passed through the tree branches. However, the Gunsmith was obviously primed for action. His hand rested on the walnut grips of his modified Colt revolver.

"I don't hear anything," Marcel whispered.

"That's what worries me," the Gunsmith answered. "There are no crickets or treefrogs chirping. That means there's someone out there."

"Could be a wolf or a mountain lion," Marcel remarked.

"In Oklahoma?" Clint shrugged. "I suppose it could be some sort of night animal, but we'd better figure it's the two-legged kind until we know for sure."

The pair waited, their muscles tense, heartbeats racing. Both prepared to draw their pistols if necessary. The silence seemed to become a sinister threat, a giant fist in a black velvet glove closing around them.

The Gunsmith was almost relieved when he saw the outline of two men, wearing stetsons and carrying rifles. The shadowy gunmen advanced quietly, trying to conceal themselves behind bushes and trees.

Since Clint and Marcel were hidden behind bushes and did not have to move, their camouflage was easier to maintain. They peered through the leaves, observing the progress of the enemy gunmen. Clint drew his revolver. Marcel's hand closed around the hilt of his sword.

The two gunmen stopped. They seemed to sense

danger. One of them pointed to the right. The other nodded. They split up, slowly drawing a circle around the area where Clint and Marcel were hidden.

Marcel looked to Clint for advice. The Frenchman was a product of New Orleans. He was accustomed to cities, streets and alleys, not the prairies and forests of the American West.

The Gunsmith pointed at Marcel and gestured at the ground, indicating that the Frenchman should remain where he was. Marcel nodded. Clint moved along a row of bushes, creeping to a thick tree trunk. He pressed himself against the rough bark and strained his eyes to try to locate one of the gunmen.

The metallic click of a lever-action weapon startled the Gunsmith. He glanced over his shoulder to see a man emerge from the bushes with a rifle pointed at the Gunsmith's back.

Marcel suddenly broke cover and charged the rifleman. The outlaw whirled to confront the new, unexpected threat. A blur of steel whirled and the flat of the blade struck the gunman's rifle, deflecting the gun barrel. The killer triggered his weapon. A .44-40 slug plowed into the ground as the report of the Winchester bellowed through the night.

The Frenchman swung his sword in a fast roundhouse sweep. The blade hissed as it sliced flesh under the outlaw's chin. The gunman dropped his rifle and clamped both hands to his throat. Blood gushed between his fingers. His eyes bulged as he wilted and fell to the ground.

Clint heard another sinister click. He pivoted and swung his Colt toward the sound. The Gunsmith saw the second gunman with a rifle aimed at Marcel. Clint fired two double-action rounds at the assassin.

A pair of .45-caliber projectiles smashed into the outlaw's upper torso. The bullets kicked him off his feet and threw him backward to collide with a tree trunk. The man slid down the wooden pillar and landed on his backside. The gunman appeared to have simply sat down and fallen asleep. Of course, he would never awake again.

"That wasn't so hard after all," Marcel remarked cheerfully as he wiped his sword on his dead opponent's shirt.

"Might not be over yet," Clint warned.

Lead missiles sizzled through the air near the Gunsmith and Marcel Duboir. Rifles cracked like metallic barks from steel-barreled hellhounds. Bullets chipped bark from tree trunks and powdered dirt near the two men's feet.

Clint and the Frenchman dove to the ground and rolled beneath the foliage of a clump of large ferns. Bullets sliced through the leaves above them. Marcel muttered something in French.

"Do you always have to be right?" he complained.

"Be careful with that sword," Clint said. "You almost stabbed me when you dove in here."

"I'm always careful," the Frenchman replied. "What do we do now?"

"The second team seems to be coming at us from the east," the Gunsmith stated. "You roll out and get to cover behind the closest tree. I'll cover you."

Marcel went into a rapid roll away from the ferns. The Gunsmith fired two rapid shots in the general direction of the unseen gunmen.

A rifle slug slammed into the ground near Clint's position. Marcel fired back at the outlaws with his Colt. Two bullets splintered the tree trunk where the Frenchman had fled to cover. The enemies' rifles roared as the outlaws drew closer.

Clint aimed carefully at the muzzle flash of one of the aggressors' weapons. A shriek of agony told Clint he'd nailed another opponent with a 230-grain messenger of death. The Gunsmith immediately scrambled from his position.

Bullets vengefully tore into the ferns. Clint hadn't abandoned his cover a moment too soon. The outlaws shot the hell out of the area. Shredded plants hopped from the fern cluster and fell like tree leaves in late autumn.

The Gunsmith darted to the cover of a pair of scrawny trees. A bullet smacked into bark, and the tree quivered violently. The bullet had punched clean through.

Clint triggered his Colt, firing a hasty round at the gunmen to encourage them to keep their heads down. Clint squeezed the trigger again. A dull click of the hammer striking the firing pin was the only response.

The Gunsmith cursed softly, annoyed that he had failed to keep track of the number of bullets he had fired. With the empty pistol in his fist, Clint bolted to a column of bushes and hurled himself into the foliage. He crashed through the thin branches and landed on the ground hard.

"He's outta ammo!" a voice shouted. "Get the bastard afore he can reload!"

Two or three gunmen opened fire on Marcel's position to pin down the Frenchman while three other killers charged toward Clint's hiding place. The Gunsmith clenched his teeth and swallowed hard. There was only one choice of action available to him and it offered only a slim chance for survival.

"Don't shoot 'im, boys," a voice chuckled. "Adams and me got some things to jaw 'bout first."

The speaker sounded vaguely familiar. Clint peeked through the branches of the bush and saw three men rushing forward. He only glimpsed the face of a large, burly figure, which Clint recognized as Lonny Sterling, the bully Clint had thrashed in the Piercetown Saloon.

"Come on out, Adams," Sterling urged with a snicker in his voice. "We know your gun is empty. Don't make it hard on yourself."

"Let's talk a deal," Clint called out as he opened the loading gate of his revolver and hastily worked the plunger to eject the spent shell casings one by one.

"Throw out your gun and stand up, Adams," Sterling ordered.

"I've got two thousand dollars back in Piercetown," Clint said, stalling for time. He reached for the cartridges on his belt. "I'll show you where—"

"Bullshit!" Sterling snapped. "Let's blast that fuckin' bush and the Gunsmith with it!"

"Wait!" Clint shouted as he reluctantly tossed the empty .45 revolver into the open. "I give up. Just don't shoot me until you hear me out."

"We ain't gonna shoot you, Adams," Sterling laughed. "You got my word on that."

Clint was surprised that the outlaws didn't simply blast him as he stepped out from the bush. Sterling grinned at Clint. He stood between two hard-faced gunmen who aimed their carbines at the Gunsmith. Sterling laid down his rifle.

"You and that Frenchy bastard beat me up in the saloon, Adams," Sterling began, distorting the actual details of the fight. "But you ain't gonna be able to hit me with a chair from behind this time."

The outlaw drew a bowie knife from its belt sheath. Moonlight danced on the foot-long steel blade. Sterling smiled as he unbuckled his gunbelt and allowed it to drop to the ground.

"I'm gonna cut you up, Adams," Sterling declared. "I'm gonna have you beggin' us to put a bullet in your head."

"You do that and you won't get your hands on that two thousand dollars," the Gunsmith warned.

"That's crap," Sterling snorted.

"Maybe not," one of the other outlaws remarked.

"Shut up, Pete," Sterling growled. "Adams is givin' us a bunch of wind tryin' to stall for time."

"I can prove I'm telling the truth," Clint declared. "I'll show you a receipt I got from the Governor for a three-thousand-dollar reward. I've already spent part of it, but—"

The Gunsmith reached inside his shirt.

"Hold it," Pete snapped. "No tricks, Adams."

"No tricks," Clint replied with a confused innocence in the tone of his voice.

Then he pulled out the .22-caliber New Line Colt and immediately shot Pete in the face. The outlaw collapsed with a tiny bullet hole in his forehead.

Clint swung the New Line toward the other gun-toting hootowl and fired two bullets into the man's chest. The outlaw staggered backward and triggered his Henry carbine. A .44 slug knifed through the bush at Clint's left hip. The Gunsmith pumped a .22 round through the side of his opponent's skull.

As the second outlaw crumbled lifeless to the ground, Lonny Sterling leaped at Clint. The unexpected impact knocked the New Line Colt from Clint's grasp. Sterling snarled like a rabid wolf as he struck at Clint with the bowie in his fist.

The Gunsmith seized Sterling's wrist above the thrusting knife with one hand, grabbed the man's shirt front with the other and fell backward. As his buttocks touched the ground, his right boot rose to meet Sterling's abdomen. Clint rolled backward and straightened his knee.

Lonny Sterling cried out in alarm as he sailed head over heels and crashed to the ground hard. Clint scrambled to his feet, scooping up a fistful of dirt as he rose. Sterling got up, his eyes ablaze with bestial fury as he charged once more with his bowie prepared for a slashing attack.

The Gunsmith hurled some dirt in his opponent's face. Lonny bellowed with rage as the dust struck his eyes and mouth. He swung his knife wildly. Clint easily avoided the blade and caught Sterling's wrist in his right hand.

Clint's left fist slammed into the side of Sterling's jaw. The outlaw's head pivoted from the punch. The Gunsmith quickly grabbed the man's forearm near the elbow and pushed down with both hands, smashing Sterling's arm across a bent knee. Bone cracked and Sterling howled as the knife fell from limp fingers.

The Gunsmith had broken his right arm.

The outlaw drove his left fist into Clint's face. The Gunsmith lost his grip on Sterling's injured arm. Sterling clutched his broken right arm and stuffed it inside his shirt to serve as an improvised sling.

The Gunsmith threw a right cross at Sterling's face. The outlaw blocked the punch with his left forearm, unaware that this was exactly what Clint had hoped he'd do. The Gunsmith's right hand grabbed the hootowl's sleeve to immobilize Sterling's good arm.

Clint delivered a quick left hook to the outlaw's broken arm. Sterling shrieked with pain. The Gunsmith kicked the man in the right kneecap before the outlaw could launch a kick of his own. Clint hammered another left hook to Sterling's broken arm and kicked him in the other knee.

The outlaw struggled violently and his left shirt sleeve ripped. Clint quickly hit Sterling with a left to the jaw, followed by a right uppercut. Sterling fell backward and staggered into a tree.

The outlaw was rough. He pushed himself away from the tree trunk and stumbled toward the Gunsmith. Sterling swung a clumsy roundhouse left at Clint's head. The Gunsmith easily dodged the outlaw's fist and punched his opponent in the left kidney. Clint hammered the bottom of his fist between Sterling's shoulder blades. The blow propelled him face-first into the tree trunk. Sterling slumped to the ground, unconscious.

The Gunsmith dashed to the bodies of the two outlaws he had slain with the .22 New Line Colt. Clint grabbed the first gun he could find. It was a Henry carbine. He worked the lever to jack a fresh cartridge in the chamber and turned his attention on Marcel's position.

The Frenchman had been busy trying to hold three gunmen at bay. However, Marcel's revolver had run out of ammo, and the enemy trio charged his position. They circled the tree, expecting to find Marcel cowering behind the trunk.

He wasn't there.

Before the baffled outlaws could figure out this mystery, a bolt of metal lightning struck from the branches of the tree. Sharp steel lanced the side of an outlaw's neck, punching through flesh and muscle to burst skin at the opposite side of the man's neck.

"He climbed the goddamn tree!" one of the outlaws cried out as he swung his rifle toward the branches.

His surviving partner was faster. He fired into the leafy foliage overhead. A bullet snapped through the treetop without striking flesh. The outlaw cursed softly as he pumped the lever of his carbine.

Marcel Duboir suddenly swung down from a limb and hurtled toward the outlaw like a human cannonball. He dove feet-first into his opponent, striking the carbine from the man's grasp. Both men tumbled to the ground.

"I got him!" the other outlaw exclaimed as he shifted his rifle toward the Frenchman's new position.

The Gunsmith gazed through the sights of the confiscated Henry carbine, and squeezed the trigger. A .44 lead projectile smashed into the back of the gunman's skull. The outlaw's face exploded when the bullet made its nasty exit where the man's nose had been.

Marcel and the last outlaw rose from the ground. The hootowl reached for his sidearm. The Frenchman stepped forward and dropped low, placing his palms on the ground as he lashed out with one leg. The sweep-kick clipped the outlaw's ankles and literally "swept" him off his feet.

The outlaw grunted as he landed on his back. He managed to clear leather, but Marcel's boot stamped the man's wrist, pinning his gunhand to the ground before he could use his weapon. Marcel's other foot kicked the pistol from his opponent's hand.

Desperate, the outlaw tried to grab Marcel's ankle. The Frenchman's foot lashed out, kicking the man's groping fingers aside. Then he ground his heel into the outlaw's throat. The outlaw's body convulsed wildly for a few moments before it lay still and accepted the ultimate judgement of death.

"Are you all right, Marcel?" the Gunsmith inquired as he approached his friend.

"*Oui, mon ami,*" the Frenchman replied. "For a moment I thought I was going to have my ticket punched to Boot Hill as you might say out here. Eh?"

"I don't think I would ever say something like that regardless of where I might be," the Gunsmith grimaced. "But it looks like we took care of everybody Harlow and Black sent after us."

"What about the rest of the gang?" Marcel asked.

"They'll either figure this business has cost too many lives already and decide to move on," Clint answered, "or they'll wait until dawn and continue to track us down by daylight."

"How long before daybreak?" Marcel wondered, gazing up at the sky.

"Less time than we had before," the Gunsmith answered. "Let's get our weapons, reload and get the hell out."

TWENTY-FOUR

The Gunsmith and Marcel Duboir returned to Pierce-town an hour after sunrise. The community which had formerly seemed so drab to the Gunsmith was now a welcome sight. Clint and his companion eagerly walked to the town limits as fast as their aching feet allowed.

The pair were burdened with weapons. In addition to the Gunsmith's modified .45 Colt revolver and his .22-caliber belly gun, Clint also carried a Winchester carbine and an ammunition belt slung over his shoulder. Marcel still carried his Colt and cane sword. He had added a Henry repeater and another .45 pistol thrust in his belt to his personal weaponry.

However, the pair had not needed this extra firepower. After the first attack by the outlaws led by Lonny Sterling, Clint and Marcel had not encountered any of Harlow's crew or Black's outlaw gang.

"I see 'em!" a voice shouted. "They made it back!"

Charlie Spotted-Horse appeared from his livery stable and waved at Clint and Marcel. Soon Sheriff Greyelk joined him. Several other townsfolk emerged from buildings and watched the pair approach Piercetown, but none of these felt obliged to greet the Gunsmith and his companion.

"We were wonderin' if you fellas got yourselves killed out there," Greyelk told Clint and Marcel.

"Not quite," the Frenchman replied dryly.

"Where'd you pick up all that extra hardware?" Charlie inquired.

"This stuff?" Clint asked as he handed the hostler the Winchester. "Some fellas we met on our way here let us have it."

"Reckon them fellas don't need them guns no more, eh?" Greyelk mused.

"We thought we might need the spare weapons and ammunition," Marcel replied. "But after our first run-in with Harlow's gunmen there wasn't a second encounter."

"How many did you have to fight off?" Charlie wanted to know.

"Eight," Clint said casually. "But that might not be the end of it."

"What do you mean?" Greyelk asked with a frown.

"There's a chance Harlow and Black will figure out we headed for Piercetown," Clint replied. "After all, it's the closest place to run to and Black already knew Marcel and I had been here before."

"You reckon they'd actually attack the town?" the sheriff shook his head. "They're probably gonna be lickin' their wounds for a while, and they can't have too many men left now."

"You said it yourself, Sheriff," Clint reminded him. "Blackie's gang could tear Piercetown apart. Could be the outlaws figure they'll do exactly that."

"Jumpin' Jesus," Charlie gasped. "And I ain't got a single stick of dynamite left."

"How many of the bastards you reckon are left?" the lawman asked. "We must've killed about a dozen of 'em all together."

"Ambushing twenty men is easier than fighting ten head on," the Gunsmith warned. "And we can only guess how many hootowls are still alive and kicking."

"You think we can organize some kind'a citizens' militia here?" Greyelk asked, shaking his head with dismay. "Most of the folks here are tired old people. They're half-breeds from half-a-dozen different Indian tribes. The only thing any of them have in common is that their people have been bullied either by whites or other Indian tribes."

"But you are a half-breed, *oui*?" Marcel remarked. "And I am one-quarter Cherokee myself."

"But you were raised as a white man," Greyelk stated. "I'm half Cree, and I was raised right here in Oklahoma so I understand this territory, and I understand the folks who live in Piercetown. They wound up here because they wanted some peace. They never learned to fight, and they're tired of being pushed around."

"They may have to fight," the Gunsmith sighed. "Unless they're so tired they're willing to just roll over and die."

"They might just do that," Greyelk warned.

"We'll try to direct the fighting to one area to minimize the risk to the townsfolk," Clint said. "But there's no way we can know how they'll hit Piercetown."

143

"One of the most simple principles of combat is if you can attack an opponent from more than one direction, you do so," Marcel commented. "I'm sure Harlow and Black realize this."

"Yeah," Clint agreed. "If they attack, they'll almost certainly surround the town. These wooden houses wouldn't be hard to set fire to either."

"My God," Greyelk said. "What are we going to do?"

"We have to come up with a plan that will be flexible enough to use regardless of what sort of tactics they use," Clint replied, "and one that will allow us to spring some surprises of our own."

"And how is this plan gonna work?" the sheriff wanted to know.

"Well," the Gunsmith shrugged. "I haven't exactly got that figured out just yet."

TWENTY-FIVE

The citizens of Piercetown assembled in the middle of the street. Sheriff Greyelk explained the possible threat of an assault by a large, ruthless outlaw gang. The townsfolk were naturally horrified by this news.

"We didn't have this kinda trouble afore these outsiders arrived," a shriveled old man declared in a reedy voice. "I say we should run 'em outta town and their women with 'em."

"If we leave Piercetown it may or may not spare you folks from Harlow and Black," the Gunsmith declared. "If you tell the outlaws we aren't here, they'll search anyway. If they don't find us, they may decide to burn down your town just for spite."

"Besides," Marcel added, "the *cochons* may not bother to ask questions. Harlow and Black are the type who prefer direct action, *oui*? They may simply attack the town without warning."

"Like the sheriff and Charlie done to Paradise," a plump, red-faced man with a necklace of colored beads complained. "You didn't have no business doin' that, Sheriff. Paradise ain't in your jurisdiction, and we had no quarrel with those whoremongers or Blackie's gang until now. You weren't thinkin' of the best interests of our community when you done that, Sheriff."

"Captain Harlow was holding innocent women captive," Greyelk replied. "Women he kidnapped so he could sell 'em like cattle on the white slavery trade. Last night those bastards murdered four of the women in cold blood. Now, I reckon that's wrong—"

"They are white men selling white women," the fat man with the beads insisted. "How is this our problem? What has the white man done for us?"

"What are you so upset about, Ephraim?" Charlie Spotted-Horse snapped. "You're a Pawnee. Your ancestors were cannibals and my ancestors, the Ogala Sioux, fought the Pawnee to make sure they never got a taste for human flesh again."

"I am not a Pawnee," Ephraim snapped. "I'm a Crow."

"You're a liar," Charlie hissed.

"Wait a minute, Charlie," Harlan, the bartender began. "Even if Ephraim is a Pawnee, I ain't heard of nobody who knows for sure that that old legend 'bout them bein' cannibals is true."

"I'd expect that from a Navajo," somebody muttered.

"I'll have you know I'm a Kiowa," Harlan snapped, whirling to confront his accuser. "And I can prove it. Kiowa are the only type of Indians that can hold their liquor worth a shit!"

"Holy shit," Clint groaned. "What got these jaspers stirred up?"

"Probably never figured Indian cultures, customs and religion vary much from one tribe or another," Sheriff Greyelk remarked. "But they sure as hell do."

"Must've been a good reason," Charlie insisted. "Especially when it comes to Pawnee—"

"Oh, shut up," Greyelk snapped. "You started this mess."

The townsfolk continued to bicker and accuse one another of being descended from murderers, cowards, and horse thieves. The Gunsmith drew his Colt and fired two rounds into the sky.

"Listen up," Clint began as he slid his revolver into its holster. "You're fighting with each other because you're scared."

"You callin' us cowards, white eyes?" a middle-aged man with a proud, fierce face demanded. "Nobody calls a Seminole a coward. My people never surrendered to the white man—"

"I'm not calling anyone a coward," the Gunsmith explained. "I'm trying to get you folks to realize that now isn't the time to fight among yourselves. "We've probably got damn little time to prepare for an attack on this community. You'll all get a chance to get a bellyful of fighting then."

"But this ain't our fight," Ephraim declared.

"They're attacking your town," Clint said. "That makes it your fight. If most of you folks want Marcel and I to leave with the three ladies who were rescued from Paradise, we'll go. However, if we leave, you'll lose our fighting skills as well."

147

"I don't reckon we can let that happen," Greyelk commented. "We can't afford to lose you, Clint. You're the best man we could have against them varmints."

"Thanks for the praise," the Gunsmith replied. "But it'll take more than one man to defeat a gang of outlaws like the one Harlow and Black have put together. We're all going to have to work together if we want to survive. Understand?"

"You're the expert, Clint," Charlie declared. "What should we do?"

"Well, you fellas have been talking a lot about your Indian heritage," Clint began. "But how many of you really know anything about fighting like Indians?"

"Hell," Harlan snorted, "we're civilized now. We're all half-white, and we live like white men."

"Yeah," Charlie Spotted-Horse commented. "Most of us have gotten fat and lazy tucked away at this graveyard that pretends to be a town."

"Well, this is Resurrection Day," the Gunsmith announced, "and we're running out of time. I want to know how many of you have used a bow and arrow, firearms, tomahawks, or any other kind of weapon."

"Tomahawks and arrows against guns?" Greyelk frowned. "What the hell do you have in mind, Clint?"

"Just a basic principle of fighting," the Gunsmith answered. "Always do the unexpected."

TWENTY-SIX

Penny, Eve and Janis were waiting for the Gunsmith and Marcel Duboir at the hotel lobby. Although the women smiled at the two men, Clint felt a cold shiver travel up his spine. He wondered how much Penny and Eve might have shared about their experiences with the Gunsmith.

"Thank God," Eve said with relief. "We were so worried about you both."

"As you can see," Marcel grinned, "we have returned safe and sound. However, although we would like to enjoy this reunion, I'm afraid none of us can spare the time just yet."

"We heard you talking to the townsfolk out there," Eve said with a nod. "So the nightmare with Harlow isn't over yet."

"I think we'll have one more confrontation before this is over," the Gunsmith admitted. "But it'll be the last."

"We heard you trying to organize a militia out there," Penny said. "Do you honestly think that collection of tired old fossils are a match for Harlow and his crew?"

"Those tired old fossils are the only hope we have," Clint answered, "and I think they'll fight to protect this town. It may not seem like much to us, but to those folks this place is home."

"I guess you're right, Clint," Penny agreed. "But I don't know if that'll be enough against those cutthroats."

"We'll soon find out," the Gunsmith replied. "Now, all we can do is get ready for trouble. Do all three of you ladies know how to use a rifle?"

They replied in the affirmative.

"Good," Clint nodded. "We'll station you at windows here at the hotel. We'll need to get each of you at least one rifle and plenty of ammunition. You should also get several buckets of water and some blankets."

"Water and blankets?" Eve frowned. "What for?"

"In case they try to burn the building," the Gunsmith answered.

"My God," Janis gasped. "Do you really think they'd do that?"

"Of course they would," Marcel answered. "They kidnapped, raped, and tortured you ladies. They would have sold you into white slavery. Harlow's people murdered at least four women. You think they'll hesitate to set fire to this entire town, *mon cheri*?"

"Tell us what we have to do," Eve said in a firm voice.

"We'll help you prepare," Clint answered. "And I'll be here at the hotel to help you fight."

"Where will you be, Marcel?" Janis asked.

"I'll be helping the sheriff and a few of the others,"

the Frenchman replied. "Most of the preparations are already complete."

"We don't have any time to spare," Clint interrupted. "Harlow's gang could strike at any moment."

"Right," Marcel agreed. He kissed Janis lightly on the mouth. "When this is over, *mon cheri,* I will show you why the French are so famous for *amour.*"

"A more what?" Janis asked.

"Never mind," Clint told her. "Marcel will show you later."

The Frenchman hurried from the hotel. Clint was relieved to discover all three women had rifles. Penny still had the Gunsmith's Springfield carbine and the other two had borrowed weapons from Sheriff Greyelk.

"After what we've been through," Penny said, "I don't think any of us will ever want to be without a gun again."

"Can't blame you for that," the Gunsmith replied. "You have plenty of ammunition for your weapons?"

"About three boxes each," Eve stated.

"You've been busy," Clint nodded his approval. "Right now we need to get as many buckets of water upstairs as possible. Eve and Janis, go out to the pump and start filling buckets and taking them upstairs. Penny, you collect as many blankets from the rooms as you can find."

The two sisters headed for the rear of the hotel to the water pump. Penny waited until they were gone before she spoke to Clint.

"Eve is quite taken with you, Clint," Penny began in a quiet voice. "She talks about you like a woman in love. I take it you and she got to be good friends after you rescued her?"

"Penny," the Gunsmith sighed, "I'm not going to argue about anything right now. There isn't time. I'm not going to try to explain anything or try to defend or justify my actions. Right now all of us have to concentrate on survival. We'll talk about personal matters later."

"But we will talk about them?" Penny insisted.

"We'll talk," the Gunsmith assured her. He didn't tell her that all he would probably say would be "good-bye."

Clint Adams wasn't a hard-hearted man, but he couldn't have a lasting relationship with a woman. The Gunsmith had accepted the fact his reputation would always haunt him. One day it would probably cost him his life.

Clint had seen more than forty years. He figured he'd used up a lot of luck already. The Gunsmith had become accustomed to his independent, uncommitted lifestyle. He had accepted the reality that it was the only way he could live.

The first rule of life is survival. The Gunsmith decided he'd better follow his own advice and get ready for Harlow's gang.

TWENTY-SEVEN

"I don't think those sons of bitches are ever going to attack this town," Sheriff Greyelk complained.

"Will you be disappointed if they don't?" the Gunsmith asked.

Greyelk had crossed the street to the hotel and found the Gunsmith in the lobby. The sheriff was becoming impatient. He and the other townsfolk had been waiting at their chosen battle stations for hours. The sky was slowly becoming darker as twilight approached.

"You reckon we'll have to stay up all night waiting for Harlow's crew?" Greyelk asked.

"I don't know how Harlow will decide to attack," Clint replied. "He might wait until after dark or even until tomorrow."

"Or he might not attack at all." The lawman clucked his tongue with disgust. "I can't keep everybody in the whole damn town standin' guard duty like this was some kinda army post.''

"You'd better maintain discipline," Clint warned. ''Especially right now.''

"What does that mean?" Greyelk demanded.

"Two of the best times to attack a target are at dusk and daybreak," the Gunsmith explained. "Dusk is coming up right now."

"Seems to me an attack would work better at night," the sheriff said. "Darkness covers your actions better."

"People tend to figure an attack will occur either at daytime or at night, right?" Clint stated. "So they figure the few minutes between light and darkness are safe. That means daybreak and dusk.''

"I never heard such horseshit," Greyelk muttered.

"Happens to be true," the Gunsmith warned. "Folks are wide awake and able to see clearly at daytime, and alert and fearful at night, but they can get damn careless in between.''

"I doubt that Harlow and Black ever heard of that fool notion," the sheriff insisted.

"I wouldn't count on that," Clint said. "It isn't exactly a state secret, and both of those fellas have enough experience to know something about fighting."

"All right," Greyelk sighed. "I'll go check on the men and make sure everybody stays alert, but I still think your theory is horseshit.''

The lawman opened the door, stepped outside and promptly received a bullet in the center of his chest. The harsh report of a rifle rung from beyond the town limits. Sheriff Greyelk's body fell back against the doorjamb and slid to the plankwalk.

The Gunsmith dragged Greyelk across the threshold. Another projectile splintered the doorframe. Clint dragged the sheriff beyond the line of fire and checked Greyelk's pulse. He found none.

"Shit," the Gunsmith muttered as he pressed two fingers to Greyelk's eyelids and gently pushed them shut.

"I hope the rest of you people aren't so careless," Clint whispered.

The Gunsmith moved to the door and quickly reached out to grab the knob and yank it shut. A lead projectile shattered glass from the door window. Clint recoiled from the door and drew his .45 Colt.

Clint crouched low as he scrambled to another window. He cautiously peered outside and saw several outlaws on horseback gallop into Piercetown. Several other enemy gunmen approached on foot.

"Two-prong attack," Clint thought aloud. "A combination cavalry and infantry attack. Clever bastards."

The outlaws fired their weapons, methodically supplying cover fire for one another. Clint didn't recognize any of the attackers. Neither Harlow nor Black were the sort to lead their men into battle. The Gunsmith hadn't figured they would.

Only a few firearms jutted from the windows of buildings to fire back at the invaders. This wasn't because the citizens of Piercetown were timid—at least, Clint hoped that wasn't the reason. If everyone was following his plan, the defenders would not attempt to beat the outlaws in a shooting match. Then, the odds would be on the side of the aggressors.

However, Clint couldn't be sure whether the townsfolk were following orders or too scared to fire at the bandits.

Worse, he couldn't be certain if the men armed with silent weapons had gone into action yet.

The Gunsmith had discovered several townsfolk were skilled with bow and arrow. Some were also familiar with tomahawks and knives. Clint had instructed these quiet killers to keep their weapons ready. If the outlaws attacked, the bowmen were under order to wait until most of the invaders had entered the town. Then they were supposed to fire their arrows at the bandits at the rear.

Since arrows are silent and bows don't emit a muzzle flash, the archers would be able to dispatch opponents without drawing much attention to their location. This made it difficult for the outlaws to know where the sniper-bowmen were located, but it also made it equally difficult for Clint to be certain if the tactic had worked.

"Clint!" Eve called down from the stairs above. "We're under attack!"

"Yeah," he shouted up to her. "Stay at your post and keep your head down. The same goes for the other women."

The Gunsmith turned his attention back to the window. A snarling bearded face stared back at him. The outlaw held a Remington revolver in his fist, thumb on the hammer to cock it back. Clint's double-action pistol fired first. A .45 caliber hole appeared in the glass pane. Another crimson hole about the same size bisected the bandit's forehead. The man collapsed on the plankwalk outside.

The door burst open, propelled by the force of a hard kick. Two outlaws leaped into the hotel lobby. One hit the floor in a fast roll across the room while his partner remained at the doorway, prepared to supply cover fire.

The pair had a pretty good system. It would have been too much for most men to deal with. Even most professional gunfighters wouldn't have been able to handle such a situation. Unfortunately for the outlaw pair, they were pitted against the Gunsmith.

Clint's modified Colt roared and a .45 bullet slammed into the bridge of the nose on the face of the man at the doorway, rearranging his brains fatally.

The Gunsmith whirled and fired two double-action rounds into the hurtling form of the bandit who was still rolling across the floor. The man's body kept tumbling until it hit a wall. By then it was already a corpse.

Clint knelt by the door and quickly removed the spent cartridge casings from the cylinder of his revolver. The Gunsmith glanced outside. The defenders were shooting back with more zeal. A number of dead bandits already lay in the street. Clint saw one bastard tumble from his saddle with at least one bullet in his chest.

Few of the outlaws remained on horseback. Most had dismounted and headed for cover at the alleys between buildings. The Gunsmith smiled. If the defenders were following orders, the hootowls would find little shelter in those alleys.

From the Gunsmith's limited viewpoint, he saw the window of the doctor's office on the second story of a building above the general store slide open. Doc Jakes placed the rim of a bucket on the window sill and poured a steaming liquid into the alley below.

Clint wondered what sort of concoction the doctor had come up with. The townsfolk in rooms over-looking alleys had been told to boil up whatever sort of nasty brew they could. Something which would do damage to human flesh. Some boiled lye or cooking oil. Harlan the bartender said he planned to fill a bucket with a combination of red-eye and his own urine and heat it up.

Whatever liquid Doc Jakes had mixed for the occasion, it sure did the job. The stuff splashed two outlaws who had fled into the alley. The pair shrieked and dropped their guns. The bandits bolted into the street, clawing at their faces and eyes.

Rifle slugs ripped into the pair and ended their suffering forever. The howls of other scalded victims informed the Gunsmith that the tactic had claimed other bandits throughout the town.

"Well," Clint mused. "I'd sure say this battle has officially started."

TWENTY-EIGHT

The Gunsmith fed fresh shells into the cylinder of his revolver as he watched the carnage in the streets of Pierce-town. At least a dozen outlaws had already been put out of action and lay dead or wounded. Clint didn't know how many defenders had been victims of the battle, but it looked like Harlow and Black were losing more men.

At least, Clint Adams hoped so.

However, there were still plenty of bandits alive and kicking among the opposition. Several hootowls had lit torches and dashed toward buildings, trying to get close enough to hurl their flaming sticks.

Two cutthroats charged straight for the hotel, firing pistols as they brandished their torches. The Gunsmith snap-aimed and squeezed the trigger of his modified Colt. A 230-grain projectile punched through an outlaw's chest and burrowed into his heart. The man collapsed in the street. His torch landed beside him, igniting his hair and beard.

The second bandit hurled his torch at the entrance of the hotel. The Gunsmith's Colt snarled. The torch split in two when a bullet sliced through it. The burning wood fell harmlessly to the ground.

The man who had thrown the torch threw down his handgun. "I've had enough! I surrender!"

He raised his hands to show his sincerity. Suddenly, he executed a macabre and clumsy dance of death when two bullets plowed into his back. The man fell, face-first in the dust. The Gunsmith glimpsed a figure clad entirely in black as it darted along the street.

"Ain't none of you boys givin' up," Edward Black snarled at the rest of the gang. "If'n we got any more cowards in the group, ya'll know what to expect if you try to quit on us!"

"Torch those bleedin' buildin's!" Captain Harlow's voice bellowed from somewhere in the shadows. "What the 'ell are you lads waitin' for?"

Two bandits tried to carry out his order. They ran toward the sheriff's office, wielding torches and pistols. A third hootowl joined the pair, armed with a Winchester for backup.

They almost reached their destination before Marcel Duboir emerged from the office with a side-by-side Greener shotgun in his fists. The Frenchman triggered the double-barreled cannon. A blast of buckshot ripped the closest man's chest to bits. The impact hurled the outlaw's corpse six feet backward.

Marcel swung the shotgun toward the rifleman and fired the second barrel. Pellets smashed into the bandit's face and burst his skull like a ripe melon struck by a sledgehammer. However, the third outlaw closed in fast and aimed his pistol at the Frenchman.

Clint Adams had long ago decided Marcel Duboir led a charmed life. The Frenchman's luck held up. He whirled and threw the empty shotgun at his opponent. The man tried to dodge the Greener, but the edge of the butt-stock struck his hand and knocked the pistol from his grasp.

The outlaw grabbed the torch in both hands and attacked, hoping to drive the flaming end into Marcel's face. Marcel let him get closer and reached for his sword. Steel flashed. The torch hopped into the air when the blade chopped through its shaft.

Marcel quickly thrust the tip of his sword under the man's ribs. The outlaw screamed and doubled up, clutching his wound. Marcel yanked the blade from his opponent's body and swiftly lashed a high roundhouse kick to the man's face. The bandit fell unconscious, dead on the plankwalk.

An outlaw raised a rifle to his shoulder and aimed the weapon at Marcel. The Gunsmith's Colt fired and the outlaw's body jerked as a bullet struck the base of his neck, severing the spinal cord. He died before he wilted to the ground.

Marcel dove back inside the sheriff's office. Bullets smashed into the walls and doorframe. Clint hoped the Frenchman's luck held up throughout the battle. He also wished Marcel would quit being so damn reckless.

A flaming projectile sizzled through the night toward the hotel like a vengeful comet. The fire arrow struck a wall somewhere above Clint's position.

''The bastards have their own arrows,'' Clint muttered,

wondering if his bowmen had carried out their assignment with any degree of success.

Clint heard water splash against the wall above. One of the women upstairs had tossed the contents of a bucket against the building to put out the fire arrow.

Another flaming arrow struck the side of the saloon. Harlan, the bartender, leaned his bulky body out a second story window and hurled the contents of a bucket at the fire. Unfortunately, he had grabbed the wrong bucket.

Instead of water, Harlan threw his red-eye and urine combination on the burning arrow. The alcohol ignited violently and flames burst along the side of the building. Harlan recoiled from the sudden blaze. His upper torso slid over the edge of the window sill. The bartender screamed in terror as his body plunged to the street below.

The Gunsmith spotted one of the enemy bowmen. The outlaw had tied an oil-soaked rag to the broadhead of an arrow and struck a match. He notched the arrow to a bowstring and prepared to draw the bow to launch his fiery messenger of destruction.

Clint gripped his modified Colt with both hands and cocked the hammer for greater accuracy. He knew the enemy bowman was out of range. The Gunsmith aimed a bit high, hoping the trajectory of the bullet would sail in a high arch and descend into his target.

He squeezed the trigger.

The bullet struck the ground near the outlaw bowman's feet, and dust spat up harmlessly in front of him. The man jumped away from it with alarm. He prepared to draw back the bowstring once again.

Suddenly, the outlaw dropped his weapon. His arms flapped wildly like a panic-stricken bird unable to fly. He fell to his knees and dropped his forehead to the ground. The shaft of an arrow jutted from between his shoulder blades like a tiny banner.

"Well," Clint thought aloud, "at least one of our bow-and-arrow boys is still alive."

Clint saw the archer stationed on the roof of the saloon. The man was a half-breed Comanche named Joshua Two Mules. He drew his compact bow and aimed at the outlaws below. Joshua released the bowstring and sent an arrow rocketing down at the enemies in the street. A bandit tumbled to the dust, an arrow driven clean through his neck.

The flames continued to spread across the saloon. The fire cast a bright, yellow light on Joshua Two Mules as he notched another arrow. Two or three outlaws saw the half-breed and opened fire.

At least one bullet hit Joshua. His body pivoted and fell backward. He tumbled off the edge of the roof and hurtled to the ground below. Joshua did not utter a sound as he fell. Clint hoped that meant he was already dead before he hit.

The crack of breaking wood and the sound of something striking a wall hard drew Clint's attention to the opposite side of the lobby. Two gunmen had kicked in the side door and rushed inside. They darted to the front desk and dove behind it for shelter.

Clint fired a hasty round into the side panel of the desk and scrambled to the only cover available: the corpse of one of the outlaws.

A gunman popped up like a jack-in-the-box from behind the desk. He aimed his six-gun at the position where Clint had been seconds before. The man was surprised to find the Gunsmith had disappeared. Clint snap-aimed and fired his Colt. The man's stetson whirled off his head. So did part of his skull.

The second gunman bounced up and fired a shot at the Gunsmith. The bullet struck the dead flesh of Clint's cover. The Gunsmith fired back and saw a crimson spider appear at the man's shoulder.

The gunman groaned and bolted for the side exit. Clint pointed his Colt and squeezed the trigger. The hammer struck the firing pin and drove it into an empty chamber. The Gunsmith switched the Colt to his left hand and quickly scooped up the corpse's .44 Remington revolver.

The outlaw reached the doorway. Clint cocked the Remington as he aimed the single-action six-shooter. The Gunsmith squeezed the trigger. A .44 slug slammed into the man's back, just below the left shoulder blade. The bullet tunneled into the outlaw's heart. He tumbled outside and died.

The Gunsmith kept the Remington close at hand as he opened the loading gate of his double-action Colt. He ejected the spent cartridge casings and reloaded. Clint thrust the Remington into his belt for a back-up pistol and moved to the side door.

He checked the alley outside to be certain no more outlaws were lurking there. Then he closed the door and jammed the back of a chair under the knob to discourage any future intruders. Clint headed back to the front door and peered outside to see how the battle had progressed.

The fighting had become more personal, more savage. The outlaws appeared to have exhausted ammunition for their long guns. They wielded pistols and empty rifles held as clubs. Close quarters combat filled the streets as bandits exchanged pistol shots with defenders and grappled with opponents in hand-to-hand fighting.

A muscular, middle-aged, half-breed Kiowa named Jim Sinsata, clashed with an outlaw near the livery stable. Armed with only a shovel, Jim struck out with the tool while his opponent wielded an empty Winchester with both fists clenched around the barrel. Jim raised the shovel to block a butt-stroke with the shaft and quickly shoved his adversary.

The outlaw staggered, trying to retain his balance. Jim grabbed the shovel like a club and swung the metal blade into the bandit's face. The outlaw fell dazed and landed on his back. Jim thrust the shovel blade under the fallen man's chin and shoved with all his might.

Blood squirted from the bandit's throat and mouth. He cried out in victory and turned to confront two pistol-packing outlaws.

"Red bastard," one of the pair hissed as he pumped a bullet into Jim's belly.

Suddenly, the first bandit threw up his arms as if about to jump with joy. Instead, he crashed face-first to the ground. The handle of a tomahawk protruded from his back like a wooden tumor.

The other outlaw whirled to face the new threat. He turned just in time to catch a bowie knife with his chest. The bandit gasped in pain as he fell to one knee and stared up at his assailant.

Charlie Spotted-Horse held another knife in his right hand. An extra tomahawk and two more knives were thrust in his belt. Charlie's face had been converted into a fierce warriors mask by war paint which streaked the half-breed Sioux Indian's wrinkled features.

The outlaw raised his pistol and tried to thumb back the hammer. Charlie's hand flashed. The bandit shrieked when the point of a second bowie knife pierced the muscles of his upper arm. The blade sunk into his biceps, and the revolver fell from his fingers.

Charlie advanced quickly and drew his tomahawk. The outlaw gazed up in horror as the half-breed hostler swung his tomahawk. The blade struck the top of the bandit's head and split his skull.

A bandit moved along the plankwalk in front of the sheriff's office, a revolver held ready in his fist. Marcel Duboir leaped outside and thrust his sword in an upward lunge. The point pierced the flesh under the outlaw's chin, slicing through the hollow of his jaw, and killing him faster than a mule skinner can curse out his team.

Another figure appeared on the plankwalk. An outlaw quickly swung his rifle like an axe, aiming the butt-stock at Marcel's skull. The Frenchman dodged the attack, but he lost his grip on the haft of his sword. The outlaw swung an overhead stroke with the rifle in his fists.

Marcel sidestepped nimbly. The butt-stock split in two when it struck the edge of the plankwalk. Marcel's right leg executed a "foot-sword" stroke, the edge of his foot striking the outlaw's elbow. Marcel's fist smashed into the man's mouth and sent him back into the side of the sheriff's office.

A well-packed kick ripped the rifle out of the aggressor's hands. The outlaw shook his head to clear it as Marcel held his fists in a pugilist stance, his feet braced in a three-point balance position. Clint wondered why Marcel didn't just use the Colt revolver on his hip instead of playing games with swords and French foot-boxing.

Of course, Marcel's *savate* skills were hardly a game. The outlaw launched himself at the Frenchman. Marcel's right foot slammed a low side-kick to the man's kneecap. The outlaw stumbled. Marcel closed in and hooked a punch to his opponent's face. He folded his left leg and hopped forward, driving his knee into the man's chest.

The outlaw fell back against the wall once more. He spat blood and uttered something which was distorted due to a split lip. Then he attacked Marcel again.

The Frenchman's right foot jerked a fast, low kick. The outlaw was ready for another attempt to kick his kneecap and made a grab for Marcel's leg before he realized the tactic was a feint. Marcel took advantage of the fact the man had lowered both hands to guards his legs, and rocketed forward a high side-kick. The outlaw's head recoiled and two teeth popped from his gaping mouth. Then he fell unconscious on the plankwalk.

The Gunsmith decided it was time to join the fighting in the street. He bolted outside and darted along a plankwalk. Two outlaws had knocked a townsfolk defender to the ground and stood over their victim, kicking and stomping him to death.

"Over here, you bastards!" the Gunsmith shouted.

One man turned to receive a .45-caliber bullet in the face. He fell backward, tripped over his victim and crashed lifeless to the ground. The other man stared at the Gunsmith. His mouth fell open in awe and fear. Clint's eyes narrowed when he recognized the hootowl.

"Don't kill me, Adams!" Lonny Sterling pleaded as he dropped the revolver from his left hand. His broken right arm was in a crudely improvised sling.

"I shouldn't have let you live before, Sterling," the Gunsmith replied simply.

Then he shot Lonny Sterling through the heart.

Without warning, powerful hands seized Clint Adams from behind. His assailant swung the Gunsmith face-first into a wall. Strong fingers gripped Clint's right arm at the elbow and twisted with monstrous force.

A scream escaped from Clint's throat as he felt his bones grate and shift at the shoulder joint. His lifeless fingers opened and the Colt dropped to the plankwalk. His opponent hurled Clint to the ground.

The Gunsmith's left hand reached for the Remington in his belt. A boot stamped on his wrist, pinning it to his chest. Clint gazed up to see the ebony features of Simba smiling down at him.

"Got you now, Yankee trash-shit," the African declared as he drew a large knife with a thick, curved blade from his belt. "Now, Simba kill you!"

TWENTY-NINE

Clint Adams raised his right leg and thrust the boot between Simba's spread legs. The Bantu wheezed in gasping agony as Clint's heel crashed into his testicles. Simba's foot slipped from Clint's chest.

The Gunsmith quickly drew the Remington, holding it awkwardly by the frame in his left hand. He sat up and lashed the butt across the Bantu's jaw. Simba groaned and fell on his backside near the wall.

Clint tried to rise. Pain sliced through his right shoulder, and he fell back to the plankwalk, his head swimming in a dizzy fog. Simba shook his head hard, growled something in Bantu and lunged forward with his knife poised for attack.

The Gunsmith braced his weight on his left elbow and kicked out with both feet. His boots struck the black man's forearm, deflecting the knife lunge. Clint rolled out of

Simba's path as the Bantu threw himself to the plankwalk. Clint heard him cry out in pain.

Simba rolled over and stared at the knife hilt which jutted from his chest. He had fallen on his own knife and driven the blade deep into his flesh. Simba shook his head as if he had just broken a teacup instead of making a mistake which would cost him his life, then slumped over, dead.

The Gunsmith thrust the Remington in his belt and rose to his feet. He moaned softly as he gripped his right shoulder. The pain was terrible. What was worse, he could not move his right arm or his gunhand.

However, the shooting had ceased. The Gunsmith glanced about and saw three outlaws with their hands raised in surrender. A group of townsfolk had the bandits covered at gunpoint.

"You reckon you win, eh, Adams?" a voice laced with a British accent remarked, accompanied by the sinister triple click of a single-action revolver being cocked.

Clint glanced to the right and saw Captain Harlow appear from an alley. He still wore his sea captain jacket and cap. The saber hung from his belt and a Tranter revolver was in his fist, pointed at the Gunsmith.

"It's over, Harlow," Clint warned. "Don't be stupid, throw down that gun and surrender."

"Think you're gonna get a chance to tell how you beat ol' Captain Harlow?" the Briton snorted. "Think again, mate. If I 'ave to 'ang, I intend to take you to 'ell with me, Adams!"

"But that will still leave me alive and able to tell the world what a piece of subhuman filth you really were," a familiar voice declared cheerfully.

170

Marcel Duboir stood behind Harlow with the point of his sword pressed against the base of the captain's skull. The Briton stiffened, but he did not drop his gun.

"Just like a bloody frog to sneak up be'ind a fella," Harlow complained. "Well, you best ease off with that pig-sticker, or I'll blast your mate, Duboir."

"You kill Clint and you're a dead man, Captain *Cochon*," the Frenchman warned. "But if you put down that gun, I'll give you a chance to die with honor. Perhaps you'll even get to kill me, if you know how to use that saber."

"You challenging me to a duel?" Harlow scoffed. "That skinny cane sword wouldn't last five seconds against a saber. Blade ain't thick enough."

"So what have you got to lose, Captain?" Marcel inquired. "Drop the gun and step into the street."

"How do I know you won't kill me as soon as I drop the gun?" Harlow demanded.

"Because I want to see your face when I kill you, Captain," Marcel hissed. "I want to smell your fear as I cut you to ribbons."

"You could do that without fightin' me," Harlow commented.

"Murder is your style," the Frenchman declared. "Not mine."

The Briton eased the hammer of his Tranter forward to uncock the revolver. He dropped it to the plankwalk. Harlow stepped onto the dirt street, and Marcel followed him.

"There's Harlow!" Charlie Spotted-Horse declared. "Let's get the bastard!"

A group of townsfolk rushed forward to seize the captain. Marcel waved his sword at the crowd and they came to an abrupt halt.

"He's mine!" the Frenchman announced. "Stay out of this. It is between the *cochon* and I. Understand?"

"Marcel," Clint began. "There's no need for this."

"I would think you'd understand, *mon ami*," Marcel replied.

"I understand," the Gunsmith assured him. "Good luck, my friend."

"*Merci*," Marcel replied as he unbuckled his gunbelt. "And you might take a look at my pistol, Clint. The damn thing jammed at the beginning of the battle."

He tossed the gunbelt aside. Harlow pulled his saber from its scabbard. Marcel's cane sword seemed spindly compared to the thick fighting blade. Harlow smiled as he slowly advanced.

"All right, frog," he snorted. "Let's see who gets to die this time."

The Briton charged. Marcel blocked the saber blade with his sword and lunged. Harlow's saber brushed the sword aside and flowed into a fast slash. Marcel turned his wrist and parried the attack with his blade.

Blades clashed again with a primitive ring of metal. Harlow swung an overhead stroke. Marcel blocked the attack with his sword and thrust a side-kick to the Briton's abdomen. Harlow staggered backward, but still managed to parry Marcel's next sword stroke with his own blade.

"No rules, eh?" the Briton chuckled. "That be fine by me, froggie—"

He slashed out with the saber. Marcel blocked the blade, but Harlow grabbed his sleeve with a free hand and pulled Marcel off balance. The Briton thrust his head forward and butted Marcel in the face with his forehead. Harlow snapped his right arm up and punched the Frenchman, his fist still clenched around the haft of his saber.

Marcel fell backward into a hitching rail. Blood oozed from his nostrils and the corner of his mouth. Harlow swung his saber with murderous force. Marcel's blade rose in time to block the thicker blade. The Frenchman's left hand grasped the rail for a brace as he swung a high roundhouse kick to the side of Harlow's head.

The Briton staggered away from Marcel. The two men squared off once more. Blades rang violently. Harlow blocked a sword thrust and shoved down with his saber to immobilize Marcel's weapon as he suddenly charged into the Frenchman like an enraged bull.

Harlow's momentum sent both both hurtling into the front window of the hotel. Glass exploded. Marcel and Harlow toppled through the opening and tumbled into the hotel lobby. The Gunsmith and several others rushed to the door to watch the duel reach its conclusion.

Both Harlow and Marcel climbed to their feet and continued to slash and thrust with their lethal blades. Harlow slammed the flat of his saber against Marcel's sword and swung a solid left hook to the Frenchman's jaw. Marcel stumbled backward into the front desk.

Harlow lunged forward and felt his saber strike home. His pleasure became alarm when he realized he had just stabbed the panel of the desk. Marcel had rolled backward on the top of the counter.

The Briton slashed a high stroke at the Frenchman.

Marcel's sword met the saber blade and he quickly punted a boot into Harlow's face. The captain staggered away from the desk. Blood dripped into his beard.

"Fuckin' frog bastard," the Briton hissed as Marcel hopped down from the desk to face his opponent once more.

The captain gripped his saber in both hands and bellowed with bestial fury as he delivered a wild, but powerful sword stroke. Marcel dodged the blade and slashed a quick cut to Harlow's midsection. The Briton swung another wild slash. Marcel leaped away from it.

Blood oozed from Harlow's torn shirt. Yet the Briton smiled and swung a third two-fisted saber stroke. This time his blade struck Marcel's sword. Metal rang sharply. Marcel jumped back from his opponent, clutching only six inches of steel in his fist.

"Told you 'bout that skinny blade, froggie," Harlow sneered. "Now, I'm gonna cut you in half, mate."

The Briton feinted a downward swing and suddenly slashed at Marcel's neck, trying to decapitate the Frenchman. Marcel ducked under the blade and dove forward. His body low, the Frenchman thrust out his right arm as he hurtled into his opponent.

Harlow screamed. He dropped his saber and fell back against the doorjamb. The half of Marcel's cane sword protruded just below his belt buckle. Six inches of steel had been driven into the captain's belly.

"My God, it 'urts!" Harlow exclaimed. "For God's sake, finish me off somebody!"

"Let him suffer," Charlie Spotted-Horse spat with contempt.

The Gunsmith stepped forward and cocked the hammer

of his Remington. He placed the muzzle against the side of Harlow's head.

"Everybody has suffered enough already," Clint announced, then he squeezed the trigger.

THIRTY

"You are leaving, *mon ami*?" Marcel Duboir inquired as he watched Clint Adams and Charlie Spotted-Horse hitch the team to the Gunsmith's wagon.

"Yes," Clint replied. "I'm heading to Kansas. Penny is riding back with me. She figures she'll be safer traveling with me than on a stagecoach."

"She does not know you very well, eh?" Marcel laughed. "But I am sorry to see you go."

"Hell, you'll be all right, Marcel," the Gunsmith said as he craddled his right arm with his left and grimaced when he moved his fingers. "You're going to be the acting sheriff here in Piercetown until they can have an election. You might even get to like it."

"Me? A lawman?" Marcel rolled his eyes. *"Merde alors!"*

"I figure you'll stay here to keep the Bayer sisters company if for no other reason."

"Oui," the Frenchman nodded. "That has an appeal for me. Yet, I am worried about your arm, *mon ami.*"

The Gunsmith's right arm was in a sling. Doc Jakes had assured him that his shoulder was only dislocated. The doctor had shifted the joint back into place, but he warned Clint to try not to use his arm for a couple days.

"It'll be fine, Marcel," Clint shrugged.

"Perhaps I worry too much," Marcel sighed. "But Edward Black's body was not among the dead."

"Black doesn't have a gang anymore," the Gunsmith replied. "Most of his men were killed last night. Blackie is probably high-tailing his way to Mexico by now. Let the *federales* worry about the son of a bitch. You just look after yourself, Marcel."

"And you do the same, *mon ami,*" the Frenchman replied. "I hope we'll meet again sometime."

"Me too," the Gunsmith agreed with a smile.

Clint Adams held the reins in his left fist as he sat in the driver's seat of his wagon. Penny sat beside him as the wagon rolled along the dirt road at an easy pace. Duke, the great black Arabian, followed the rig, tied to a guideline at the rear of the wagon.

"Well, Clint," Penny remarked. "We sure had quite an adventure back there at Piercetown and Paradise."

"Paradise isn't a place," Clint grinned, "it's a frame of mind, as the poets might say. Reckon we can find some paradise for ourselves, from time to time."

"You and me?" Penny inquired.

"I had that in mind," the Gunsmith nodded.

"Until you get involved with some other woman like Eve for example," Penny said in a stiff tone.

"I wasn't offering anything permanent," Clint shrugged. "After all, our relationship started out pretty casual."

"I suppose you're right," Penny sighed. "I can't really imagine you'd ever make a good husband. You're a hell of a man, Clint Adams, but you're not the type to settle down and get married."

"That's a fact," the Gunsmith admitted.

He stiffened when he saw a lone figure step into the middle of the road. The man was dressed entirely in black, from his stetson to his boots. A serpentine smile slithered across the outlaw's face as he looked up at the Gunsmith and rested a hand on the black grips of his holstered revolver.

"Afternoon, Adams," Edward Black greeted. "Appears to me that you and the lady are on your way to Kansas. Never cared for that state much. Too many farmers and not enough banks."

"Wondered if you'd try to bushwack me on the trail," Clint remarked as he hauled back on the reins to bring the wagon to a full stop. "Sort of figured you'd be more apt to hide somewhere with a rifle and try to dry gulch me."

"I was gonna do just that," Black admitted, "until I seen your gun arm is all crippled up. Is it broke, Adams?"

"Dislocated," the Gunsmith replied. "But it's still too stiff to quick-draw a gun, if that's what worries you."

"As a matter of fact, it is," Black confessed. "See I always knew I couldn't take you, Adams. You're faster than me. But that ain't gonna help you now, is it?"

"Clint—" Penny began.

"Shut up, bitch," the outlaw snapped. "Adams and me is gonna settle somethin', and then I'll decide whether

I'm gonna let you live or not.''

"Just stay put, Penny,'' Clint urged. "If I lose, grab the Springfield carbine and kill the bastard.''

"What did you say to her, Adams?'' Black demanded.

"I told her to watch me kill the bastard,'' the Gunsmith replied as he stepped down from the wagon. "That means you, Black.''

"We'll see who gets killed, Adams,'' Black sneered. "You got your gun with you?''

Black noticed the Gunsmith had shifted his gunbelt around his waist until the buckle was at the small of his back. The holster was positioned at his left hip, the grips of his modified Colt revolver jutting forward.

"Got your gun backwards in the holster,'' Black snorted. "Some fellas like to use it that way. You ever draw a gun from that position, Adams?''

"Sometimes,'' the Gunsmith answered.

"Well, now is your chance to find out if you're any good that way,'' Black said as he patted the black grips of his sidearm. "Make your move, Gunsmith.''

"You're the one who wants to fight,'' Clint replied.

"Yep,'' the outlaw smiled. "I'm the fella what's gonna be known as the Man Who Killed the Gunsmith.''

Black yanked his revolver from its holster and thumbed back the hammer as he pointed it at the Gunsmith. A shot exploded. Edward Black staggered two steps backward and fell to his knees. Blood formed a crimson stain on his shirt front.

The Gunsmith held the modified Colt in his left fist. Smoke rose from the muzzle of the gun like incense to a god of righteous destruction.

"By the way,'' Clint remarked. "Whenever I practiced

drawing a gun from a backwards holster, it was always with the left hand.''

He fired the double-action revolver again. Black squirmed then fell face-forward in the dust. The Gunsmith calmly returned his gun to its holster.

''Never know when a skill might come in useful,'' he concluded with a shrug.

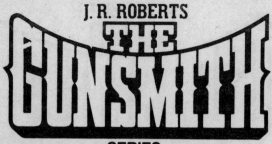

J. R. ROBERTS
THE GUNSMITH

SERIES

☐ 30928-3	THE GUNSMITH	#1: MACKLIN'S WOMEN	$2.50
☐ 30878-3	THE GUNSMITH	#2: THE CHINESE GUNMEN	$2.50
☐ 30858-9	THE GUNSMITH	#3: THE WOMAN HUNT	$2.25
☐ 30925-9	THE GUNSMITH	#5: THREE GUNS FOR GLORY	$2.50
☐ 30861-9	THE GUNSMITH	#6: LEADTOWN	$2.25
☐ 30862-7	THE GUNSMITH	#7: THE LONGHORN WAR	$2.25
☐ 30901-1	THE GUNSMITH	#8: QUANAH'S REVENGE	$2.50
☐ 30923-2	THE GUNSMITH	#9: HEAVYWEIGHT GUN	$2.50
☐ 30924-0	THE GUNSMITH	#10: NEW ORLEANS FIRE	$2.50
☐ 30931-3	THE GUNSMITH	#11: ONE-HANDED GUN	$2.50
☐ 30926-7	THE GUNSMITH	#12: THE CANADIAN PAYROLL	$2.50
☐ 30927-5	THE GUNSMITH	#13: DRAW TO AN INSIDE DEATH	$2.50
☐ 30922-4	THE GUNSMITH	#14: DEAD MAN'S HAND	$2.50
☐ 30905-4	THE GUNSMITH	#15: BANDIT GOLD	$2.50
☐ 30886-4	THE GUNSMITH	#16: BUCKSKINS AND SIX-GUNS	$2.25
☐ 30907-0	THE GUNSMITH	#17: SILVER WAR	$2.50
☐ 30908-9	THE GUNSMITH	#18: HIGH NOON AT LANCASTER	$2.50
☐ 30909-7	THE GUNSMITH	#19: BANDIDO BLOOD	$2.50

Prices may be slightly higher in Canada.

Available at your local bookstore or return this form to:

CHARTER BOOKS
Book Mailing Service
P.O. Box 690, Rockville Centre, NY 11571

Please send me the titles checked above. I enclose _____. Include 75¢ for postage and handling if one book is ordered; 25¢ per book for two or more not to exceed $1.75. California, Illinois, New York and Tennessee residents please add sales tax.

NAME _____

ADDRESS _____

CITY _____ STATE/ZIP _____

(allow six weeks for delivery.)   A1

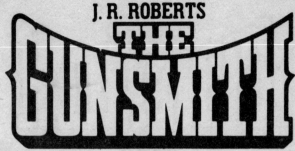

THE GUNSMITH

SERIES